The Shattered Doctor

A SHERLOCK HOLMES MYSTERY

MARC HILL

smoky coast

SMOKY COAST PRESS

Cover design by Marc Hill
Printed in the United States of America

Publisher's Cataloging-in-Publication Data (Prepared by Smoky Coast LLC)
Hill, Marc, 1980-
The Shattered Doctor / Marc Hill. -- First edition.
p. cm.
ISBN 978-1-968057-08-4 (paperback)
ISBN 978-1-968057-06-0 (hardcover)
ISBN 978-1-968057-07-7 (ebook)

Library of Congress Control Number: 2025923429
1. Holmes, Sherlock (Fictitious character)--Fiction. 2. Watson, John H. (Fictitious character)--Fiction. 3. Private investigators--England-- London--Fiction. 4. Post-traumatic stress disorder--Fiction. 5. Psychological fiction. 6. Historical fiction. I. Title.
PS3608.I4567 S53 2025   813'.6

For permissions, inquiries, or rights, please contact:
Marc Hill or Smoky Coast LLC at smokycoastllc@gmail.com

First Edition

Dedication

I dedicate this book to my daughters: Annika, Piper, and Cora.

Always strive to accomplish your dreams no matter what challenges lie before you.

Stay positive and keep pushing forward!

Contents

Introduction

London never forgets. Its cobbled streets hold memory like bone holds ache—quietly, constantly. You can try to wash the blood away, but it always leaves a stain of history.

This Holmes story came from a single question that I wouldn't let go: What if the man Sherlock Holmes trusted more than any other was the very one he could not save? From there, the cracks widened. What if war had done more to Watson than we knew? What if the wounds he carried were more dangerous than anyone realized? And what if someone with a sharp mind and no soul saw those fractures... and decided to twist the knife?

I wrote this book not just as a tribute to Sir Arthur Conan Doyle's world—but as a way to pull back the curtain on the shadows behind it. Holmes and Watson were never just puzzle-solvers. They were men in a broken world trying to make sense of chaos. This story asks what happens when even that brilliance isn't enough—when evil is systemic, coordinated, and wears the face of medicine, government, and even friendship.

You'll find real threads of history here. The Ripper murders. The turmoil of veterans returning from British colonial wars. The political rot at the edges of empire. Every date and murder in the background lines up with the real autumn of 1888. But woven between the facts is fiction—dark and deliberate, grounded in the psychology of trauma and the brutal machinery of manipulation.

This isn't a clean mystery. It's not a tidy caper. It's about the slow corrosion of trust and identity—and what it costs a man to lose his grip on both.

And yet, through the smoke, one thing remains: friendship. Fragile, complex, and harder to kill than most people think. This will not be your average ordinary Holmes story.

Thank you for stepping into the fog with me.

—*M. H.*

CHAPTER 1

A Stranger in the Fog

T he urgent ring of the front bell shattered the quiet night.

It rang once, twice, then again—with the persistence of desperation. I had been lying restlessly in bed, the pain in my hip and shoulder a constant reminder of the shrapnel that could not be found, aching with each shifting gust of the late-summer storm that had broken over London. Beyond thunder rolled across the rooftops like distant cannon, and my mind traveled back to the war in Afghanistan, as it always did when sleep had eluded me.

From the sitting room below, Holmes pacing footsteps was a steady rhythm against the floorboards. "But why? For what possible reason?" His aggressive voice drifted up through the thin walls, followed by the plucking of strings on his violin. The Sholto case had consumed him completely for the past fortnight; something complicated in the legacy of the Indian Agra treasure was perplexing him.

The bell rang again, more insistent now.

I threw on my housecoat, the floorboards frigid against my bare feet as I made my way downstairs. Sergeant Whitehead stood on our threshold, soaked to the bone, his helmet dripping steadily onto his blue overcoat. He'd ridden hard through the storm to reach us.

"Sorry to call so late, Doctor," he said, glancing over my shoulder as Holmes materialized behind me. "We've got another one. North Woolwich. Fished a man out of the river about an hour past."

Holmes stepped into view, his hair disheveled, but his eyes already sharpened to distinctive intensity. "The Thames has been particularly hungry of late Sergeant."

"Aye, no wounds we can see, sir. And no signs of struggle neither. But Inspector Bradstreet, he figured Mr. Holmes might take an interest." Whitehead shifted uncomfortably, water pooling at his feet. "Thing is, sir, the body... well, it's been stripped. Boots, coat, most everything of value. But not robbed, if you take my meaning. More like...prepared."

Holmes's eyebrows lifted slightly. "Prepared? An interesting choice of words."

Within moments we were dressed and bundled into the police cab. The early morning streets were dead, emptied by the storm. Fog had rolled in heavily from the river, muffling the world to only what you could slightly see five paces ahead.

"Another laudanum case," Holmes mused, settling back against the damp leather seat. "The sergeant was less than convinced."

"You heard something in his voice too?" I adjusted my medical bag, old habits from campaign days—always know where your instruments are.

"Uncertainty. Fear, perhaps." Holmes paused, looking out and studying the fog-shrouded streets. "If Bradstreet's bringing us into this..."

The cab jolted over treacherous cobblestones. I found myself drifting back to Afghanistan again—the copper taste of blood, the endless parade of broken bodies under my hands. How many had I saved? How many had I lost? The faces blurred together now, a gallery of the living and the dead.

The body was waiting for us at the water's edge, surrounded by a loose circle of Metropolitan Police officers who parted respectfully as Holmes and I approached. Even in the wavering lantern light, I could see why Whitehead had been disturbed.

The corpse lay face-down, limbs twisted in a peculiar way pointing to a violent struggle with death itself. The sergeant was correct; the man had been stripped of his clothing, leaving him in only his undergarments and a thin cotton shirt clung to his pale flesh like a burial shroud. He'd been in the water long enough for the Thames to begin its grim work—skin gone waxy and pale, hair slicked to his skull like murky oil.

Inspector Bradstreet approached us, his usually immaculate uniform rumpled and damp. "Mr. Holmes, Dr. Watson. Body was found washed up about midnight. No identification, but from the look of him, I'd say he's been in the water at least four to six hours."

Holmes walked a slow circle around the scene, his eyes cataloging every detail. He crouched occasionally to examine footprints in the mud. Still, he said nothing until he kicked the dead man's shoulder—not gently—until the body rolled over with a wet, heavy sound forcing several constables to step backward in shock.

The face stared up at us was beginning to bloat, but recognizable as human, though death and the river had robbed it of dignity. The eyes were gone—fish had been at them—but something about those facial features tugged at the edges of my memory.

Holmes crouched beside the corpse and lifted one limp hand. The fingers were curled inward, as if clutching something long since lost to the deep water. He studied the palm, his nose wrinkling at the smell. The stiffness of the fingers and arm suggested time of death.

"Laudanum," he said quietly. "Opium. dead fish, of course." He inhaled more deeply. "And underneath...something bitter. What would you say, Watson?"

I stepped closer, every instinct screaming at me to maintain distance. The smell was complex—opiates mixed with the Thames's particular bouquet of sewage and decay. "Metal," I said finally. "Something metallic. Iron, perhaps, or copper. But something sweeter underneath it all, like a flower maybe."

"Interesting." Holmes released the dead man's hand, brushing his hands on his handkerchief. "No bruising on the throat or wrists. No ligature marks. No wallet, no coat, no boots. No facial hair to speak of, and his cut is short, bearing military involvement. Stripped, yes, but not robbed in the conventional sense."

"Overdose then?" Bradstreet asked hopefully.

Holmes was quiet for a long moment, studying the body with peculiar intensity. "Obvious enough," he said, but something in his tone suggested the obviousness troubled him. "Poorly cut opium, taken in excess. The bitter smell suggests it was mixed with something else—probably to stretch the dose."

He paused, then added with a dismissive wave, "Not particularly interesting, I'm afraid. The Thames claims a dozen such victims each month."

But even as he spoke, I found myself staring at the dead man's face. The bone structure, the set of the jaw, the way the hair lay against the skull—all of it whispered of someone I had known.

In the wavering light of the police lanterns, with shadows playing across the corpse's features, recognition hit me like a lightening bolt. The slightly crooked nose, broken in some childhood accident. The small scar above the left eyebrow.

"Simon?" I whispered softly.

I knelt beside the body, my medical training taking over even as my heart hammered against my chest. With gentle fingers, I brushed away wet hair and examined the ruined face of a man I had known.

Private Simon Bailey. The young lad who had trusted me to heal him.

"What was that, Doctor?" Whitehead leaned in closer.

"Simon Bailey. Private, 5th Northumberland Fusiliers. I operated on him at the Battle of Maiwand." The memories flooded back—Bailey screaming and gripping my wrist as I cut into him, the sound of shells falling around our makeshift field hospital, the thickness of cordite, blood, and fear.

I reached for his shirt and pulled it up gently. There it was, three inches below the left shoulder—a long, crescent-shaped scar, faded but unmistakably mine. The field incision I had made in the dirt and chaos.

"My God," I breathed. As I struggled to stand, my hip protesting, Bailey's voice shot through my mind: "You're saving me, Doctor. I can feel you saving me."

But I hadn't saved him, had I? I had merely postponed this moment, delayed his appointment with death by a handful of years.

When I searched for Holmes, hoping to share this revelation, he had vanished into the fog as completely as if he had never been there at all.

Whitehead produced a grey blanket and draped it over Simon Bailey's remains. I bowed my head and said a quiet prayer—for Bailey's soul, for forgiveness. For all the men I couldn't save, all the wounds I couldn't heal, all the promises I couldn't keep.

"Did he have family, Doctor?" Whitehead asked gently.

"I don't know," I admitted. "I should have known. I should have..."

But what should I have done? Tracked down every man I'd treated in Afghanistan?

As the police began their grim work, I stepped back and stood alone in the fog, wondering how many other Simon Baileys were out there, drifting through London like ghosts of a war the Empire preferred to forget. How many were struggling with similar hidden wounds?

The following afternoon, I found myself unable to concentrate on my medical practice. Every patient who sat across from my desk blurred into Bailey's waterlogged face. Mrs. Hudson had noticed my distraction, remarking with her usual directness I was "rather out of sorts today, Doctor."

Holmes had been his usual infuriating self at breakfast, buried behind his newspaper and showing no interest in discussing the previous night's events. When I'd attempted to bring up Bailey's military service, he'd merely grunted. "The Yard will handle it adequately, Watson. We have more pressing matters."

More pressing matters. As if a man's life—and death—could be dismissed so easily.

I left my practice early and found myself walking aimlessly through London's afternoon bustle. The storm had passed, leaving puddles reflecting the pale blue sky, but I couldn't shake the image of Bailey's crescent-shaped scar beneath his shoulder. How many times have I traced similar marks on other patients? How many men carried my handiwork on their flesh?

Lost in these shadowy reflections, I almost walked past the pawn-shop entirely. It was only a flash of familiar crimson in the window grabbing my attention and bringing me to a sudden stop.

There, hanging between a tarnished silver pocket watch and a lady's silk parasol, was a military tunic. The faded red wool with a green inseam was unmistakably of the 5th Northumberland Fusiliers, the brass buttons dulled by time but bearing the regimental insignia.

It couldn't be. But something about the cut of the shoulders, the way the fabric had faded, made my heart begin to race.

I stood transfixed by the possibility fate had placed this particular item in my path. I let out a deep sigh and I pushed open the shop door as the bell rang above my head.

The shop's interior smelled of mildew and pipe smoke. Behind the counter sat a thin man with graying hair and spectacles perched on his nose. He looked up from a ledger as I entered, his expression shifting to something approaching suspicion.

"The military coat in the window," I said. "I'd like to inspect it."

He studied me for a moment, then nodded and moved toward the display. "Came in yesterday. Some pretty girl dropped it off, didn't even haggle for a price. Said she needed the money quick-like." He held up the garment to the light. "Good quality wool, this. Afghan campaign, I'd say."

The moment my fingers touched the fabric, I knew. This wasn't any Fusilier's tunic—this was Bailey's. The lining was worn where his shoulder blades had rubbed, and there, inside the collar, careful hand-stitching: S.B., embroidered in precise lettering.

"The girl who brought it in," I said, trying to keep my voice casual. "Did she say where she got it?"

"Didn't ask. Pretty thing, well-dressed, but nervous-like. Had an accent—Irish or Welsh maybe. Kept looking over her shoulder." He leaned in closer. "Between you and me, I got the feeling she wasn't supposed to be selling it. But I don't ask questions you know, might complicate my business."

The coat was still slightly damp, and when I lifted it closer, I caught the faint scent of the Thames. Someone had taken it from Bailey's body, perhaps even before he'd fully died.

"How much?"

He named his price—probably twice what he'd paid the girl—but I didn't argue. I flipped him a shilling, he caught with skillful ease in midair.

As I turned to leave, coat folded over my arm, he called after me. "Military man yourself?"

"Yes. Afghanistan."

He sternly nodded as if it explained everything.

I stepped back into the afternoon light, Bailey's coat heavy in my arms. The street had changed, as though the discovery had twisted the world's geometry upon itself. It was only when I reached the street corner I felt it—a small, hard lump in the left lower pocket.

I carefully reached inside, my fingers closing around a familiar form. I pulled out a misshapen piece of metal, tarnished but unmistakable.

The bullet I had extracted from Bailey's shoulder all those years ago. The souvenir I had given him with a jest about the Queen's service. He had kept it all this time, carrying it like a talisman.

I stood on the busy London street, holding the crude piece of metal, and felt something break inside my chest. The weight of it was enormous—not the physical burden, but the weight of all the questions it carried.

The lead bullet was warm in my palm, and I felt Bailey's presence in it. His trust, his gratitude, his hope for a future ultimately denied to him.

I slipped the bullet into my waistcoat pocket, close to my own heart, and folded Bailey's coat more carefully over my arm. As I resumed my walk back toward Baker Street, my mind was already racing ahead, formulating plans.

Holmes might consider this case beneath his notice, but I could not. I owed Bailey more than that. I owed him the truth about how he had died, and why.

I climbed the seventeen steps to our shared quarters, each one a small effort reminding me how thoroughly the events of the past day had drained me. Holmes was in the sitting room, surrounded by what appeared to be the explosion of a small library. Papers covered every available surface—maps of India, shipping manifests, genealogical charts, and page after page of his precise handwriting.

Holmes' took in my disheveled appearance and the military coat. For a moment, I thought he might comment, might show some flicker of interest. Instead, he merely nodded.

"Ah, Watson. Perfect timing. I believe I've finally cracked the essential pattern in the Sholto correspondence." He held up a sheet covered with complex cipher work. "The treasure wasn't hidden in Agra at all—it was brought to London, piece by piece, over several years."

I stood there, Bailey's coat draped over my arm, and felt something cold settle in my stomach. Here was Holmes, brilliant as always, completely absorbed in his intellectual challenge. And there I was, holding the possessions of a dead soldier, burning with questions.

"The man's name was Simon Bailey," I said quietly. "I operated on him. Maiwand, 1880."

Holmes finally raised his head from his papers, his expression mildly curious. "You recognized him? Remarkable, considering the state the Thames had left him in."

"I recognized the scar I gave him." I moved to the window, needing distance from his casual dismissal. "He kept the bullet, Holmes. The one I removed. Carried it with him all these years."

"Soldiers often keep such mementos. A tangible reminder of their survival." His attention was already drifting back to his documents. "Though in this particular case, rather ironic."

The callousness hit me like a slap across my face. I pivoted from the window to face him fully. "This man trusted me to save his life. I succeeded then—got the bullet out clean, sewed him up properly.

And now I find him dead in the Thames, stripped of everything but his undergarments."

"A not uncommon fate for veterans, I'm afraid." Holmes didn't look up from his cipher. "The mind has its own wounds, Watson."

"Someone took his coat. His boots, his personal effects. But not to rob him—they left his shirt, his trousers. Why strip a man and then leave him half-clothed?"

For the first time, Holmes gave my words genuine consideration. He set down his pen and leaned back in his chair, steepling his fingers. "You're suggesting there was something specific they were looking for?"

"I'm suggesting someone wanted it to look like a simple overdose and robbery, but weren't quite careful enough." I held up Bailey's coat. "I found this in a pawnshop on Drury Lane. Still damp from the Thames. The shopkeeper said a nervous young woman brought it in yesterday morning with an accent, well-dressed, wouldn't haggle."

Holmes's eyebrows rose slightly. "You bought a Deadman's coat?"

"I bought the coat of a soldier I once saved." I pulled out the mis-shapen bullet. "And I found this in the pocket. The same bullet I extracted from him in war."

Holmes studied the bullet without speaking, his mind cataloging details. Finally, he nodded slowly. "An interesting development. Though I continue to maintain the fundamental circumstances point to accidental overdose."

"Or someone making sure there was nothing on the body to identify him or point to how he died." I set down my medical bag harder than necessary. "Holmes, I intend to look into this further. With or without your assistance."

He regarded me with what could only be described as mild surprise. "Watson, you cannot save every veteran who falls by the wayside. London is full of broken soldiers. You'll drive yourself mad trying to help them all."

"I'm not trying to help them all. I'm trying to help one."

Holmes was silent for a moment studying my face. "This is about more than Private Bailey, isn't it? This is about your own ghosts."

He wasn't wrong. The war had left its mark on me as surely as it had on Bailey, though mine were perhaps less visible. "Perhaps. But it doesn't make it less important."

Holmes nodded slowly, then returned to his papers. But I caught something—a flicker of consideration, a pause suggested his mind was filing away details despite his dismissive words.

"Very well. But I trust you won't let this personal crusade interfere with more pressing matters. The Sholto case promises to be quite lucrative, and Mrs. Hudson has been pointed about our financial obligations."

"I'll be discrete of course."

"See you are." He picked up his pen again, but then paused. "Though I will say this, Watson—if you do uncover something genuinely suspicious about Private Bailey's death, I trust you'll inform me. A consulting detective can ill afford to disregard a genuine mystery, even when it presents itself as a mere suicide."

I nodded, noting how he'd said "mere suicide" rather than "simple overdoses". Holmes was more interested than he cared to admit.

As I left the room, he spoke again without looking up. "Watson? Be careful. If someone did kill Private Bailey, they had reasons going beyond robbery. Don't assume you understand those reasons until you've examined all the evidence."

It was good advice, and I took it to heart as I hung Bailey's coat in my wardrobe. I sat on my bed and pulled out the bullet again, turning it over in my hands. Such a small thing to carry so much weight. When I had given it to Bailey all those years ago, I had meant it as a symbol of survival, of hope.

Now it felt like an accusation. But it was also a promise.

Taking out my journal I began to write down the events as best I could. I would start tomorrow with the veterans' hospital on the South Bank. Someone there would have known Bailey, would have seen him in his final weeks or months. Someone would have answers to the questions lining up to keep me awake this night.

And perhaps, in seeking justice for Simon Bailey, I might find some peace for my own troubled conscience.

Tonight, I would plan.

CHAPTER 2

The Bullet in the Pocket

I awoke the next morning to the familiar smell of coal smoke as I made my way south across London Bridge. Sleep had eluded me again. It had been nearly a week now of consistent lack of rest, but my thoughts were now filled with dreams of Bailey's waterlogged face and the weight of the misshapen bullet in my pocket. Holmes was gone when I rose, leaving only a note about pursuing some lead in the Sholto case, suiting my purposes perfectly.

My destination was Blackheath Veterans' Hospital. As I approached, it loomed before me like a fortress of brick and iron, its Gothic Revival architecture casting long shadows across the manicured grounds. The main gates stood open, flanked by stone pillars topped with carved lions watching my every step with weathered eyes.

However, I had learned from Holmes servants' entrances often yielded more honest information than the front door.

As I made my way to the rear of the hospital, it was a different world entirely—utilitarian and bustling with the quiet efficiency of those who kept the machinery of care running. Kitchen staff moved between buildings; laundry hung from lines, and the aroma of curry and sweet paprika drifted from the cooking quarters. I paused at the kitchen entrance, remembering Holmes's oft-repeated advice: "Keep quiet, Watson. Ears open. You'll be amazed by what you learn from listening."

The kitchen itself was a symphony of controlled chaos. Indian cooks worked with precision, their movements cautious and swift as they prepared what I assumed was the midday meal. Steam rose from great copper pots, and the air was thick with spices reminding me, not unpleasantly, of my time overseas. For a moment, I was transported back to field kitchens and the simple pleasure of hot food after days of hardtack and uncertainty.

"Dr. Watson? Are you lost?"

The voice behind me was stern but not unkind. I turned, surprisingly to find myself facing a middle-aged woman in the crisp white uniform of a senior nurse. Her cap was pinned with military precision, and her tone suggested someone accustomed to authority. She was attractive in a practical way, with streaks of graying hair and intelligent eyes studying me with obvious recognition.

"Well, by God, it is you! Just look at you!" Her stern expression melted into something approaching genuine warmth, though professionalism kept it in check. "It's Martha Whitmore," she said pointing at herself and extending her hand. "Though I suppose you knew me as Nurse Whitmore back in Kandahar."

Whitmore. The name unlocked a flood of memories—yes, a skilled nurse who had worked tirelessly in our makeshift hospital, someone who could keep men calm while I worked on them, who never flinched at blood or screaming. But the years had changed her as they often do, adding lines around her eyes and a certain caution born of accumulated grief.

"Nurse Whitmore," I said, shaking her hand. "I should have recognized you, I apologize. You saved more lives than any of us doctors, keeping the men steady while we worked."

"Flattery will get you nowhere, Doctor," she replied, but I caught the pleased flush in her cheeks. "Though I must say, finding you wandering about in our kitchen is unexpected. Not that you're unwelcome, mind you, but..." She gestured at the bustling activity around us.

"I'm here about Bailey," I said simply. "Simon Bailey. He was found in the Thames two nights ago."

Her expression shifted, the professional mask slipping to reveal sincere grief. "Indeed," she said quietly looking down. "Terrible thing. We only heard yesterday morning. The girls and I, we've been quite shaken by it."

She glanced around the kitchen, then gently took my arm. "Come along, Doctor. This isn't the place for such conversations."

As she led me through a maze of corridors, I noted the hospital's curious mixture of military tact and institutional decay. The floors were spotless, but paint peeled from the walls. Yet, as we passed one wing, I was struck by the sight of brand-new, expensive medical equipment being wheeled inside and installed, a stark contrast to the flickering gaslights in our own corridor. The expense appeared unusual for a publicly funded veterans' hospital. The smell was very familiar—sterilizing agent and despair, with undertones of whatever medicinal herbs and flowers they used to mask the odors of human suffering.

"That's the third lad this month," she said as we walked, her voice barely above a whisper. "I can't figure why anyone would take their clothes, boots, and such, then dump them in the river like that. Makes no sense to me. What kind of horrible creature would do such a thing?"

I stopped walking. "Three deaths? All found the same way?"

She nodded grimly. "Stripped to their undergarments, all of them. No identification, no personal effects. If we hadn't recognized the faces..." She shuddered. "Inspector Bradstreet's been by twice, but he seems to think it's a coincidence. Veterans taking too much laudanum, robbed after they died."

"But you don't think so?" I asked her.

"Doctor, I've been working with these men for over two years now. I know the signs of an overdose, and I know the signs of a man who's been... prepared for disposal." She paused at a heavy door marked 'STAFF ONLY.' "Bailey wasn't the type to take his own life, not even accidentally. He was getting better, truly he was. Dr. Shepard will tell you the same."

As I was about to ask about Dr. Shepard, she tilted her head and nodded to someone behind me. "Just a moment, Doctor."

I saw a tall, thinly built man in an orderly's clothing standing at the far end of the corridor. He had the look of a soldier, but something in his posture suggested he was waiting for instructions. Nurse Whitmore walked briskly toward him, her quick footsteps echoed in the empty hallway.

Their conversation was brief and conducted in whispers, but I caught the tension in both their postures. The orderly's eyes flicked toward me once, and for an instant I thought I saw recognition before he nodded sharply and disappeared round the corner.

When Nurse Whitmore returned, her professional smile was back in place, but I sensed an underlying current of anxiety.

"Forgive the interruption," she said. "Hospital business never stops, as you well know. Now, you mentioned you're here about Bailey. I think some men would like to see you. Would you mind coming to the day room?"

It wasn't a question; she wrapped her arm around mine, and I found myself being guided deeper into the hospital's maze of corridors. The institutional green paint reminded me uncomfortably of military hospitals, places where men were stored and counted rather than healed.

The day room was behind a heavy gate, clanging decisively as Nurse Whitmore unlocked it. The sound recalled prison doors, though I knew the comparison unfair—these men were patients, not prisoners. Still, the symbolism was hard to ignore.

Inside, the room was larger than I had expected, with tall windows meant to provide cheerful sunlight but instead filmed with years of London grey soot. Roughly ten men occupied the space—some in white hospital pajamas, others in faded red tunics and white trousers marking them as veterans clinging to their military identity. Yet it was their faces that struck me most; each bore the unmistakable expression of men who had seen too much, survived too much, and now drifted through a world with little use for their sacrifice.

I had seen the look before, in mirrors and in the eyes of other veterans. It was the look of men who had touched the edge of hell and returned, but not unchanged. It was a look I had seen in my own mirror.

"Robert!" Nurse Whitmore called out.

A young man rose from a chair near the window, using a crutch to balance for his missing left leg. He moved with the surprising speed of someone who had long ago adapted to his limitations, and as he approached, I felt a jolt of recognition.

"Well, good morning, Doc," he said, extending his hand with a grin momentarily transforming his haggard features. "Thanks for coming by."

"Corporal Robert Rode!" I exclaimed, grasping his hand warmly. "My God, man, I thought you were dead. Last I heard, you were being shipped back on the hospital train..."

Rode's smile wavered slightly. "Aye, the Deli Death Train, they called it. And you weren't wrong to think me dead—I nearly was. Fever took me for three weeks, and the infection in this leg..." He gestured at his missing limb. "But I'm still here, and that's down to you,

Doc. The surgery you did, the way you cleaned out the shrapnel—it bought me enough time to get proper treatment."

The emotion in his voice caught me off guard, and I found myself blinking back tears. How many times had I wondered about the men I'd treated in Afghanistan? How many had I assumed were lost to the war's hungry jaws?

"What brings you down here?" Rode asked, his expression growing more serious.

"I'm here to ask about Simon Bailey. Do you remember him?"

The change in the room was palpable. Conversations stopped, and several men shifted in their seats to face us. Rode's face darkened, and he glanced toward Nurse Whitmore before answering.

"Yeah, we heard about Bailey," he said quietly, looking down at the floor. "Tough loss, that. He was getting better, you know. Even Dr. Shepard thought so."

"Yes, who is Dr. Shepard?"

"He's our alienist, what they call a mental physician now. Specializes in what they're calling 'battle fatigue.' Says it's a real condition, not cowardice or weakness." Rode's voice carried a note of hope mixed with skepticism. "Been working with most of us for the better part of a year."

Both Rode and Nurse Whitmore exchanged a look when he mentioned Dr. Shepard's name, and I caught something in their expressions—a tension showing there was more to the story than they were willing to share.

"How has Dr. Shepard been helpful?" I asked carefully.

"He's... different," Rode said after a pause. "Uses new methods. Hypnosis, dream analysis, something he calls 'therapeutic catharsis.' Some of the lads swear by it, say it's helped them sleep better, stopping the nightmares. But he's always going on about his powerful friends in Parliament, some lord or another who's funding all his research and giving him the funds to help us. Says they believe the Empire must be 'pruned' of its weaknesses to remain strong."

"And what do you think?"

Rode shrugged. "I'm not sure. Sometimes I feel better after our sessions, but sometimes... sometimes I feel like I've lost pieces of myself. Like memories have been moved around, or conversations I thought never happened."

A loud voice cut across the room.

"Well, this is a pleasure indeed."

I was amazed to see a short, rotund man approaching us with quick, deliberate steps. He wore a well-tailored suit hanging loosely on his frame, and thick spectacles enlarging his pale eyes. His receding hairline lent him a scholarly air, though the intensity in his face reminded me of Holmes when he was upon the scent of a particularly intriguing case.

Behind him walked the same orderly I had seen in the corridor, maintaining a respectable distance but serving as some sort of escort or bodyguard.

"Dr. Shepard, I presume?" I said, extending my hand.

"Indeed, and you must be the famous Dr. John Watson. I've been wanting to meet you for quite some time." His handshake was firm but brief, and his smile never quite reached his eyes. "Your reputation precedes you, both as a physician and as the chronicler of Mr. Holmes's adventures. The men here speak of you with great respect—many are alive because of your skill."

"You're too kind, Dr. Shepard. I understand you've been working with these men on their psychological wounds?"

"Precisely. The mind, Dr. Watson, is far more fragile than we previously understood. The traumas of war leave invisible scars, but no less real than physical wounds. I've been pioneering new treatments based on the latest Continental research."

"And Bailey was one of your patients?"

Shepard's expression grew somber. "Indeed, and his death is a terrible tragedy. I felt we were making genuine progress. He was beginning to confront his demons, to understand the root causes of his distress."

"What can you tell me about his final weeks?"

For a moment, something flickered in Shepard's eyes—calculation, perhaps, or suspicion. "He was struggling, as many of our patients do. The transition from military to civilian life is never easy, especially for men who've seen combat. Bailey, although had been self-medicating with laudanum, it's unfortunately common among veterans."

"Self-medicating? How was he obtaining the drugs?"

Shepard glanced at Nurse Whitmore, who shrank slightly under his gaze. "I'm afraid some of our patients have been... resourceful. The hospital's medication stores are carefully monitored, but determined individuals sometimes find ways to access additional supplies."

"You mean they've been stealing drugs?"

"Such a harsh word, Doctor. I prefer to think of it as a cry for help, a symptom of their underlying condition." Shepard's tone was patronizing, and I found myself disliking him intensely. "Bailey and some others had been taking extra opium and laudanum, selling what they didn't need to fund their habits."

"Selling to whom?"

"The usual suspects—dealers in Whitechapel, desperate souls who prey on the vulnerable." Shepard waved his hand dismissively. "It's a cycle as old as addiction itself."

Nurse Whitmore spoke up, her voice sharp with barely controlled anger. "Trim the tree."

The effect was immediate and startling. Shepard's head snapped toward her, and for a moment, his mild professional mask slipped to reveal something bitter and dangerous. Nurse Whitmore cast her eyes to the side, like a dog being scolded by its master.

"What did you mean by that?" I asked.

Shepard's smile returned, lacking any sincerity. "Nurse Whitmore sometimes speaks in... metaphors. She's referring to the need to remove diseased branches from society's tree—the criminals and addicts who corrupt innocent others. It's a philosophical discussion we've had about the nature of social decay."

The explanation felt rehearsed, hollow. I was about to press further when Shepard consulted his pocket watch.

"Look at the time, I'm late for my next appointment. Nurse Whitmore, could you show Dr. Watson out, please?"

"Of course, Doctor," she replied, but her voice was subdued.

As we prepared to leave, I went back to Rode. "It was good to see you, Corporal. I'm glad you made it home."

Our eyes met, and I saw something there—a desperate need to communicate something he couldn't say in front of Shepard. His mouth opened slightly, then closed again, and he simply nodded.

"Thank you for coming, Doc. It... it means more than you know."

As Nurse Whitmore led me away from the day room, I couldn't shake the feeling I had witnessed a carefully orchestrated performance. But performed for whose benefit, and to what end?

The corridor outside the day room was eerily quiet after the subdued conversations within. Nurse Whitmore walked beside me in silence, her earlier warmth replaced by a tension emanating from her bones. The encounter with Dr. Shepard had unsettled her, and I found myself wondering about the dynamics of power within this institution.

"Nurse Whitmore," I said gently, "that phrase you used—'trim the tree.' What did you mean by it?"

She glanced around nervously before answering. "It's something Dr. Shepard says during his lectures to the staff. He believes society must be... pruned of its undesirable elements. Those who are weak, who burden the system, who cannot contribute meaningfully to the Empire's strength."

"And you disagree?"

"I've spent my life caring for men who've sacrificed everything for our Empire," she said quietly. "I've seen them broken in body and spirit, then cast aside when they're no longer useful. These men should be lifted up and celebrated, Doctor. But our present government seems fit to give aid to those who should be able to help themselves. Criminals and trash who are the real 'undesirable elements' dragging our society down."

The emotion in her tone and the look in her eyes showed she meant what she said.

We had reached the main entrance hall, a grand space with marble floors and portraits of distinguished physicians staring down from the walls. The contrast between this public face of the hospital and the shabby reality I had witnessed in the day room was stark.

"Dr. Watson," she said, stopping near the door, "I want you to know not all of us agree with the extent of Dr. Shepard's methods. Some of us remember what it means to heal, not only to... manage."

"What exactly are his methods?"

She cast her eyes about once more, then stepped closer and lowered her voice. "He uses hypnosis, yes, but not just to help the men remember and process their trauma. Sometimes it seems like he's trying to make them forget things or remember them differently. And the drugs he prescribes—they're not only for pain or sleep. They make the men compliant, docile."

"For what purpose?"

"I don't rightly know. But I've seen men go into his private sessions bright and alert, and come out confused, disoriented. Bailey was one of them, toward the end. He asked if he'd spoken words he couldn't recall, if his actions belonged to dreams more than memory."

A chill ran down my spine. "How long had Bailey been under Dr. Shepard's care?"

"About six months. He came to us after a series of incidents—fights in pubs, problems with the police, the usual difficulties veterans face. Dr. Shepard took a special interest in him, said he was an ideal candidate for his research."

"Research?"

"Dr. Shepard is writing a scientific paper, something about the application of modern psychological techniques to military medicine. He's been documenting all his cases, taking detailed notes on the men's responses to his treatments."

She stiffened and moved away from me. I glanced over my shoulder to see Dr. Shepard approaching, his orderly trailing behind him like a loyal puppy.

"Dr. Watson," Shepard said with false warmth, "I hope Nurse Whitmore has been taking good care of you. I trust you found your visit illuminating?"

"Indeed," I replied carefully. "I'm beginning to understand the challenges these men face."

"Precisely. And I hope you appreciate the complexity of the work we're doing here. These men are not simply broken—they are raw material for understanding the human mind under extreme stress. Their sacrifice continues to serve the Empire, even in their current state."

The casual coldness of his words made my blood run cold. "They're human beings, Dr. Shepard, not experimental subjects."

"But idealism doesn't advance science, Dr. Watson. Results do. And my results speak for themselves."

"What results?"

"Why, the reduction in violent incidents among my patients, the improvement in their compliance with hospital regulations, the decrease in their... troublesome behaviors." He paused, studying my face. "Of course, there are occasional setbacks. Some patients prove more resistant to treatment than others. Bailey, unfortunately, was one of those cases."

"Resistant how?"

"He began to question his memories, to doubt the reality of his experiences. A common side effect of trauma, of course, made therapeutic progress difficult. He became convinced his treatment sessions were somehow altering his perceptions, which is obviously impossible." He gestured toward the entrance.

But the way he said it—with a hint of smugness—made me wonder if Bailey's concerns had been entirely unfounded.

I nodded and acknowledged his suggestion to exit. As I walked out through the entrance hall, I could feel Shepard's eyes boring into my back.

"Thank you for your time," I said loudly enough for anyone listening to hear. "I hope your work here continues to help these brave men."

Nurse Whitmore nodded, but as we reached the doors, she leaned close and whispered, "Be careful, Doctor. Dr. Shepard has... influence. And he doesn't like questions."

The front doors of the hospital banged shut behind me with an ominous finality. I stood for a moment in the afternoon sunlight, trying to process everything I had learned. The official story—Bailey had overdosed on stolen drugs and been robbed—was beginning to seem increasingly unlikely. But if it wasn't what had happened, then what was the truth?

As I walked perhaps twenty yards from the hospital entrance, I heard footsteps behind me. The orderly from Dr. Shepard's side was approaching at a quick pace, his thin frame moving with surprising stealth and speed.

"Dr. Watson," he called softly. "A moment, sir."

I stopped, my hand instinctively moving to the walking stick I carried—a habit from my military days served me well in my adventures with Holmes.

The orderly came within arm's reach and paused, his eyes scanning the area to ensure we were alone. He was even more imposing up close, with the scarred hands and weathered face of a man who knew violence. But there was something in his expression—a desperate urgency he was taking enormous risks by approaching me.

Without speaking, he pressed a small piece of folded paper into my hand, then walked quickly back toward the hospital. I watched him disappear through the gates before unfolding the note.

The message was brief, written in a careful hand:

Polly at Buck's Row.

I stared at the paper, my mind racing. Buck's Row was in Whitechapel, an area I knew by reputation if not by direct experience. It was a place where the desperate and the destitute gathered, where questions were rarely asked and answers were rarely given freely.

But who was Polly?

As I folded the note and slipped it into my waistcoat pocket, next to Bailey's bullet, I realized my investigation had taken on a new dimension. What had begun as a simple inquiry into the death of a former patient was becoming something far more complex and dangerous.

The afternoon sun was beginning to slant through the London haze, casting long shadows across the hospital grounds. I cast a final glance toward the imposing structure and wondered how many secrets it contained. How many men like Bailey had disappeared into its depths, only to emerge changed—or not at all?

The journey back to Baker Street gave me time to think, but my thoughts were troubled. Holmes had been right about one thing—this case was about more than Bailey's death. It was about the systematic destruction of men who had already sacrificed everything for their country, and about those who would exploit their suffering for personal gain.

But Holmes had been wrong about something else. This wasn't about my own ghosts, my own guilt over the men I couldn't save. This was about justice for those who had no voice, no advocate, no champion except for an aging army doctor with a limp and a conscience he couldn't quite silence.

As the cab rattled through the London streets, I found myself thinking about the cryptic message. *Polly at Buck's Row.*

Tomorrow, I will venture into Whitechapel's shadowy streets and see what secrets they hold. The game, as Holmes would say, was afoot. But this time, the stakes were more than intellectual satisfaction. This time, they were measured in the lives of broken soldiers and the honor of those who had fallen.

CHAPTER 3

At the Frying Pan

The evening fog had descended upon Whitechapel like a sulking cat, creeping through the narrow streets and alleyways with the patience of a hunter. By the time I reached Buck's Row, the world had been reduced to a series of dim circles of occasional gaslight. The darkness was home to the underbelly of London, and it was just the way they liked it.

I had never ventured so deep into the East End before, especially at this late hour and alone, and the contrast with Baker Street was stark and unsettling. Here, the air felt charged with danger. The cobblestones were slick with something more than rain. Rats scurried confidently between my feet, their eyes gleaming red, as if they were the true masters of this neighborhood.

The buildings pressed in close on either side, their upper stories leaning outward. Laundry hung from windows despite the dampness, creating ghostly shapes in the fog, startling me more than once. The local odor was overwhelming—human sewage, rotting vegetables, unwashed bodies, and underneath it all, the sickly-sweet scent of opium permeated every surface.

I felt profoundly out of place. Every step announced my foreign status to this world, and I was acutely aware of the whispered conversations taking place as I strode by. Faces appeared and disappeared in doorways, watching me with expressions ranging from wonder to outright hostility.

"Lost, are you, Guv?" A voice called from the shadows.

There in the dim light was a woman leaning against a lamppost, her painted face garish in the yellow light. She was perhaps thirty, though the hard life of the streets had aged her. Her gaudy red silk dress had seen better days, and her smile revealed several missing front teeth.

"I'm looking for someone," I said. "A woman named Polly."

Her laugh was harsh and knowing. "Polly? Which one, love? Got three Pollys on this street alone. What's she done, then? Or what's she not done?" She winked lewdly.

"She would know about the veterans from Blackheath Hospital. Men who come here for... medicine."

The woman's expression shifted, the false cheer evaporating like morning mist. "You're not from around here," she said warily. "What's your game, then?"

"No game. I'm a doctor. I'm trying to help some soldiers."

"A doctor?" She laughed again, but there was less humor in it now. "Right, then. You'll be wanting Polly Nichols. Try The Frying Pan—she's usually propping up the bar by now. But mind yourself, doc. She's got a temper, and she don't much like gentlemen asking questions."

She started toward the door, then paused and turned toward me. "And doc? Round here, helping usually means minding your own business. Just a friendly word of advice."

As I continued down the street, the warning stuck in my mind. Every face I passed carried the same message—I was an intruder here, a specimen from another world entirely. Children with hollow eyes watched me from doorways, their silence more unnerving than any hostility.

I stopped to question a group of men huddled around a small fire burning in a metal drum. They were a mixture of types—dock workers, street sweepers, and men whose occupation was impossible to determine from their appearance. When I mentioned Polly's name in connection with the hospital, they exchanged glances laden with meaning.

"Hospital lads, eh?" said one, a grizzled man with a patch over his left eye. "Yeah, they come through here regular-like. Looking for something to take the edge off, if you know what I mean."

"You mean opium?"

"Among other things." He spat into the fire, where it hissed and steamed. "Polly, she's got connections up the hill. Gets the good stuff, not the rat poison they usually peddle to the likes of us, the kind of stuff coming from people with money. "

"What kind of connections?"

The men's eyes met each other again, and I sensed I was approaching dangerous territory. The man with the eye patch leaned closer, and I caught the smell of gin on his breath.

"Listen—be careful. Prying into such business can land you in a far worse sort of trouble than a crack on the head."

One of the younger men, barely more than a teenage boy, spoke up nervously. "She works at the veteran's hospital, though. The short doctor, the fat one with the spectacles. He gives the lads their medicine, and sometimes there's extra— for sale."

The older man cuffed him across the head. "Shut your mouth, Tommy. You want to end up like—" He stopped himself, glancing at me.

"Like whom?" I pressed further.

But they were already moving away, melting back into the fog with the skill of men who knew survival often depended on disappearing at the right moment.

I was alone again on the dim street, but now I had a destination—the Frying Pan. And I had confirmation of what I had suspected—Dr. Shepard's involvement in this sordid business went far deeper than he had admitted.

The Frying Pan public house was ahead through the mist, its windows glowing with the promise of warmth and answers. But as I approached the doors, I couldn't shake the feeling I was crossing a threshold I couldn't return from. A foreboding darkness settled overhead.

The moment I pushed through the heavy wooden door, I was assaulted by a wall of sound, smoke, and human misery. The pub was crowded with bodies pressed together in a way that spoke of desperation rather than sociability.

The air was thick with tobacco smoke, ale, gin fumes, and something else, the stench of opium mingled with human sweat. Candle flames flickered against soot-stained walls, casting wavering shadows, making the faces around me appear almost demonic. The floor was sticky underfoot, layered with sawdust long since defeated in its battle against spilled drink and worse substances.

The clientele was precisely what I had expected from such an establishment in this part of London, addicts of various types, criminals, prostitutes, and those unfortunates who had fallen so far from grace that even their original occupations were no longer evident.

But it was the argument near the bar drawing my attention. A woman's voice, raised in anger and defiance, cut through the general commotion with the clarity of a razor's edge.

"You lyin' bastard! I delivered exactly what we agreed, and now you want to change terms?"

I pushed through the crowd toward the source of the commotion. The woman was perhaps forty, with auburn hair once beautiful but now hanging in chunked strands around a weathered face etched by years of hard living.

The man she was arguing with was tall and thin, and as he moved his head, the light caught his features, and I felt a jolt of familiarity. He was the orderly I had seen in the hospital corridor, the harsh dim light carving different shadows into his face, but it was undoubtedly the same man—the man who had silently pressed the note directing me to "Polly" into my hand.

What was his game? Was he a friend leading me to a source, or a foe luring me into a trap? His menacing posture now suggested the latter, and I proceeded with a heightened sense of caution as I stepped forward.

"The transaction's concluded, Polly," he said, his voice carrying a threat despite its quiet tone. "The doctor wants more discretion now. Too many questions are being asked."

"Then the doctor can bloody well pay for more discretion," she shot back. "I ain't running a charity here."

Two other men walked over and separated them. The tall man gulped the last of his ale pint and threw it down on the bar top.

"Polly Nichols, I presume?" I said, my eyes fixed not on her, but on the man, I knew was playing a dangerous double role.

She faced me, and I saw immediate suspicion in her expression. Polly's forehead narrowed as she took in my appearance.

"Who's asking?" she demanded.

"Dr. John Watson. I want to buy you a drink and ask you a few questions."

The thin man beside her tensed, but Polly held up a hand. "Wait, Eddie. Let me hear what the good doctor has to say." Her look changed to be both calculating and oddly seductive. "Questions about what, then?"

"About Simon Bailey. I believe you knew him."

The thin man, now known to be named Eddie, started to move toward me, but Polly grabbed his arm. "It's all right, love. Run along, we'll finish our business later."

He hesitated, his expression betraying his displeasure with the situation, then leaned close to whisper in her ear, prompting a grim nod. With a final hard look at me, he disappeared into the crowd with his cohorts. Yet, as he turned, his eyes met mine for a fraction of a second. I saw not the simple menace of a street tough, but a flicker of something deeper—resentment, perhaps, or a weariness. It was the look of a soldier following orders he no longer believed in.

"Well then, doctor," Polly said, her demeanor shifting to something now flirtatious, "you mentioned a drink. I'm partial to gin, if you're buying."

I waved my hand to signal the barman, a surly individual with forearms like tree trunks, who hobbled over, "Gin for the lady and whiskey for myself."

"So, you're here about poor little Simon," she said, accepting her drink with ease. "Awful thing, what happened to him. Found in the Thames, wasn't he? Stripped and robbed."

"Did you know him well?"

She shrugged, taking a generous sip of her gin. "Well, enough. He was one of the hospital lads—came down here regular-like for his medicine. Nice boy, polite and sweet. Not like some of the others."

"His medicine?"

"Don't play innocent with me, doc. You know what kind of medicine the lads need. The drugs to help them sleep without seeing their dead mates every time they close their eyes."

"Opium, you mean."

"Among other things. The doctor at Blackheath takes good care of his lads. Make sure they get what they need to stay... manageable."

"Dr. Shepard, you mean?"

Her eyes sharpened. "You know him, then? Course you do—you're cut from the same cloth, ain't you? All you medical gentlemen, thinking you know what's best for everyone."

"I'm not like Shepard."

"No?" She leaned closer, and I caught the scent of gin and something else—flowery, maybe lavender oil, perhaps, a pathetic attempt to maintain some illusion of decency. "Then why are you here, asking questions about dead soldiers? What's your game, eh?"

"Simon and I served together in the 5th Fusiliers during the war. I want to know what really happened to him."

"What really happened?" She laughed, though it carried no warmth. "He got too curious, that's what happened. Started asking questions, like you're doing now. Started wondering why some lads got better medicine than others, why some got special treatment from the good doctor."

"What kind of special treatment?"

"The kind driving a man to forget what he should remember and recall what never happened." She drained her gin in one swallow and signaled for another. "Little ol' Simon Bailey, he started talking about how his sessions with Shepard were making him feel strange. Like parts of his memory were missing."

This confirmed what Nurse Whitmore and Corporal Rode had hinted at, and I felt a chill of dread. "Did he say anything specific about what he couldn't remember?"

"Sometimes he'd wake up after a session and not know how he'd gotten back to his room. Or he'd find things in his pockets—money, little trinkets—he couldn't account for." Her face snapped toward me with a hard stare. "You're not drinking, doctor. Don't you trust the company?"

I realized I had been holding my whiskey without tasting it, too focused on her revelations to pay attention to the cheap whiskey. "Of course," I said, and took a generous sip.

The whiskey burned going down, and I noticed it had an odd, bitter aftertaste. But Polly was watching me with near glee in her eyes, and I didn't want to seem suspicious.

"Did Bailey ever mention specific incidents he thought he might have done while under Shepard's influence?"

"Oh, he mentioned things all right." Polly's second gin arrived. "Said he had dreams about hurting people, about doing evil deeds, which made him sick to think about. But were they dreams, or were they memories?"

She leaned closer, her voice dropping to a whisper. "Bailey wasn't the only one, doctor. There's been others—lads who got too curious, who started asking too many questions. They end up dead, and nobody seems to care much."

"How many others?"

"Two, three—maybe more. All found the same way. Stripped, dumped in the river, or left in alleys. All of them had been getting Shepard's special treatment."

The room was growing uncomfortably warm, and I found myself having difficulty focusing on Polly's words. The whiskey affected me more than it should have, given how little I had consumed.

"You're looking a bit peaked, doctor," Polly said, and there was something in her voice—concern mixed with something else. Something devious.

"I'm fine," I said, though I wasn't sure it was true. The faces around us began to shift and blur, and the noise of the pub was becoming buzzing and throbbing in my ears.

"Course you are." She reached out and touched my hand, her warm fingers against my skin. "Relax, doctor. Let old Polly take care of you."

Her touch was oddly comforting, and I found myself leaning toward her despite every instinct screaming that something was wrong. The room was spinning gently now, and Polly's face was the only thing in focus.

"That's it," she whispered. "Let go. Stop fighting it."

I tried to stand, knowing I needed to get out of the pub, get back to familiar territory to think clearly. I had been drugged, but my legs wouldn't support me correctly, and I found myself gripping the edge of the bar for balance.

"Easy, doctor," Polly said, her arm slipping around my waist in what anyone watching would assume was a supportive gesture. "Why don't we get you some fresh air?"

As she helped me toward the door, I caught a glimpse of Eddie walking toward us from across the room with the two other men. Polly's voice, close to my ear, "This is what the doctor ordered."

Then the world tilted sideways, and everything went dark.

I awoke to the sensation of freezing rain striking my face like tiny hammers. My head felt as though it had been split open and quickly reassembled. Every heartbeat sent waves of pain radiating from behind my eyes, and my mouth was dry and tasted strange.

I was lying on my back in an alley, surrounded by the rubbish of broken bottles, rotting vegetables, and other substances I preferred not to identify.

My first coherent thought was I had been robbed. My second was confusion at discovering my wallet and watch were in their proper places. But as I struggled to sit up, fighting waves of nausea threatening to overwhelm me, I realized something else was missing.

My walking stick—the sturdy Malacca cane, my constant companion since returning from Afghanistan—was nowhere to be found.

I examined my hands in the dim light and found them filthy; the nails caked with mud but might have been something else entirely. My clothes were disheveled and damp, and there were stains on my jacket I couldn't account for. More disturbing was the complete absence of memory regarding how I had come to be in this condition.

The last clear recollection I had was of The Frying Pan with Polly. After that, there was nothing but fragments—impressions of movement, voices, screams, fighting, and the sensation of being guided somewhere against my will. But the details remained frustratingly out of reach, like trying to grab the wind.

I managed to get to my feet, though the effort left me swaying and forced to lean against the brick wall for support. The alleyway appeared to be behind The Frying Pan, though I couldn't be certain. The buildings all had the same architecture in this part of Buck's Row.

The rain had eased, and I heard the rush of water in the gutters, carrying away the grime. A distant church bell chimes four.

I had been unconscious for nearly four hours.

As I began to make my way toward what I hoped was the mouth of the alley, I became aware of a commotion somewhere ahead. Voices rose in excitement or alarm, the sharp blast of police whistles, the sound of running feet. My training as both a physician and as

Holmes' companion had taught me to recognize the signs of disaster, and every instinct told me something terrible had happened.

The alley stretched endlessly before me, my progress hampered by my unsteady legs and the determined pounding in my head. But as I drew closer to the street ahead, the sounds became clearer. Men shouting orders, women crying, the authoritative tones of police officers trying to maintain control.

When I finally emerged from the alley, I found myself on a street I didn't recognize. A crowd had gathered around something further down the road, held back by a line of Metropolitan Police constables.

I approached the crowd slowly, my medical instincts overriding my personal discomfort. Someone had been hurt, and regardless of my own condition, I might be able to help.

"What's happened?" I asked a woman standing at the edge of the crowd.

She surveyed me, taking in my appearance with obvious distaste. "Murder," she said simply. "Poor girl's been done in proper. Cut up something terrible, they say."

Disgust and immense sadness filled my spirit. "Cut up?"

"Aye. The devils had their fun. Found her lying there like a piece of butcher's meat."

I pushed through the crowd with authority, ignoring the protests of those I moved.

"I'm a doctor," I said to the nearest constable. "Dr. John Watson. I may be able to assist."

He nodded and allowed me to pass, and I found myself looking down at a haunting sight.

The body lying in the narrow confines of Buck's Row was of a woman, though death and violence had robbed her of dignity and humanity. She lay on her back as if she had been carefully positioned. But it was the ghastly wounds that struck me, falling to my knees in the street, my stomach lurching with recognition and horror.

It was Polly.

The clinical part of my mind—the physician trained to observe and catalog even the most horrific injuries—automatically began to assess the damage done to Polly Nichols. But the human part of me, the part remembering her touch and her whispered words, recoiled from what I was seeing.

Her throat had been cut deeply, the wound extending from ear to ear in a single, devastating slash, severing the major blood vessels, and leaving her spine partially visible. But that was not the worst of it. Her abdomen had been opened like a field dressing, the incisions clean and purposeful. Her intestines had been partially withdrawn and laid across her shoulder in a deliberate arrangement rather than a frenzied attack.

The ground around her body was surprisingly clean of blood, given the seriousness of the inflicted wounds. Her clothes had been ripped but not removed—her skirt pulled up to expose the abdominal wounds; her petticoat was torn open. There was something almost ritualistic about the positioning, as if whoever had done this had been following a specific pattern.

"Dear God," I whispered.

"Dr. Watson?"

I looked up to see Inspector Bradstreet approaching, his face was pale but determined.

"Inspector," I managed, struggling to regain my composure. "I... I knew this woman."

Bradstreet's eyebrows rose slightly. "Knew how?"

"We spoke last night. At The Frying Pan. She was... she was helping me with my inquiries about Bailey's death."

"And now she's dead." Bradstreet's tone was neutral, but I caught the implication in his words. "Curious coincidence, at that."

I heard a familiar voice calling my name. Holmes was approaching through the crowd, already taking in the scene with his peculiar concentration. He was immaculately dressed despite the early hour; Inspector Bradstreet must have sent for him.

"Watson," Holmes said, his observation moving from my disturbed presence to the body and back again. "You look terrible. Are you quite well?"

"I'm fine," I lied.

Holmes studied me for a moment longer, then shifted his attention to the corpse. He circled it slowly, his hands clasped behind his back, occasionally crouching to examine specific details. His face revealed nothing of what he was thinking, but I knew his brilliant mind was cataloging and analyzing every aspect of the scene.

"Interesting," he said finally. "The wounds are surgical in nature; someone with medical training did this. The positioning is deliberate, almost ceremonial. And the timing..." He glanced at me again. "Note the depth of the incision, Watson — precise enough to avoid bone but angled to maximize blood loss. This is no accident. Only a hand accustomed to the scalpel would possess such confidence." Holmes moved to the other side of the body and had a strange look on his face. "Watson, you've seen worse than this. What about this particular death has affected you so profoundly?"

I couldn't answer. How could I explain I had been with this woman only hours before her death? I had no memory of how I had spent those missing hours. I was terrified of what I might have done while under the influence of whatever drug had been slipped into my drink.

Holmes' expression softened slightly. "Perhaps you should return to Baker Street and rest. This scene is not going anywhere, and you're clearly not yourself."

But I couldn't leave. Not yet. I found myself staring at Polly's left hand, clenched around the gate of a stable entrance at the moment of her death. Something was distressing about the gesture, as if she had been reaching for help that never came.

"Inspector," one of the constables called from across the street. "You'll want to see this."

Bradstreet crossed the narrow road to where the constable was standing beside a pile of refuse. He bent down and retrieved something, holding it up for examination.

It was the broken handle of a walking stick. Malacca wood, with silver fittings, caught the morning light.

My walking stick.

Holmes and Bradstreet's gazes fixed on me. I felt the weight of their judgment.

Holmes said in a low voice, "Watson, the odds of such an item appearing here by chance are infinitesimal. Either you placed it yourself in a state you cannot recall, or someone has staged this scene to incriminate you. In either case, you are now as much a target as the murderer."

CHAPTER 4

Dreams of Maiwand

The silence in the carriage was oppressive, broken only by the rhythmic trotting of horse hooves on cobblestone and the occasional crack of the driver's whip. Holmes sat across from me, studying my unkempt appearance with intensity.

"Watson," Holmes said finally, his voice cutting through the tension, "I think it's time you told me exactly what happened last night."

The clattering wheels sounded like distant gunfire, and for a moment, I was back in Afghanistan, listening to the artillery grow closer while Sargent Blake's voice echoed in my ears, "Keep the lights burning, Doc." I felt my heart sink as the memory dissolved into the gray London morning.

"I spoke with Polly Nichols at The Frying Pan Pub. She had information about Bailey's death."

"Yes, but what happened after the conversation?" Holmes leaned forward slightly. "You left Baker Street yesterday evening in perfect health. You return this morning looking as though you've been dragged through every gutter in Whitechapel, with no memory of the prevailing hours and your broken cane found at the murder scene."

"I don't remember," I said, though fragments drifted through my mind like smoke, the sensation of being led somewhere, voices speaking in hushed tones, the feeling of cold metal in my hand.

"Watson, you're a physician. You understand the effects of various substances on the human mind and body. What do you believe happened?"

I closed my eyes, trying to summon any coherent memory from the lost hours. The bitter taste of whiskey returned to my palate, bringing with it the phantom scent of sterilizing acid saturating every breath in our desert field hospital, where men died faster than I could save them.

"I believe I was drugged," I said slowly, opening my eyes to meet Holmes's probing gaze. "The whiskey at The Frying Pan—it had an odd taste, bitter. And Polly... she watched for some reaction."

"What kind of drug?" Holmes pressed.

"Something to render me amenable, possibly. Chloral hydrate mixed with alcohol would produce the symptoms I experienced—memory loss, disorientation, physical weakness." The clinical analysis came naturally, a refuge from the deeper fears clawing at my consciousness.

"And during this period of... compliance, what do you suppose you might have done?" Holmes quipped.

The question hung in the air like an executioner's axe over my head. Holmes examined me, waiting for an answer I couldn't give because the truth was too horrible to contemplate.

"I don't know," I whispered softly.

Holmes let out a long sigh and sat back in his seat. "The wounds on the victim were inflicted with surgical precision. The killer had medical knowledge, Watson. Considerable medical knowledge."

The words summoned the weight of my bistoury scalpel in my hand, the way its curved blade had parted flesh with practiced ease when I extracted Bailey's bullet in the sweltering tent. "There you are," I had told him, holding up the small piece of lead. "Your very own Victoria Cross—lead and pain, but you'll live to tell the tale." Bailey had managed a weak smile despite his wounds, grateful for the liberation. How different was healing from the opposite? How thin is the line between cutting to save and cutting to destroy?

"You can't seriously believe—"

"I believe in evidence and deduction," Holmes interrupted. "And the evidence suggests whoever killed Polly Nichols possessed skills few men in London can claim. And you, my dear Watson, are one of those men."

"As is any surgeon in the city. Why focus suspicions on me?"

"Because you were the last person seen with the victim. Because your walking stick was found at the scene. And because you have no alibi for the time of her death."

The carriage lurched to a stop outside 221B Baker Street, but none of us moved to get out. The weight pressed down on me, making it difficult to breathe, like the crushing sensation I had felt beneath the rubble at Maiwand when the world had collapsed around me and death seemed inevitable.

"There's something else," Holmes said quietly. "Something I haven't mentioned yet."

I lifted my eyes to him, dreading what he might say next.

"The arrangement of the body," he continued. "It wasn't random violence, Watson. It was deliberate, methodical. And there's a pattern to it—something suggests the killer was following a specific procedure or purpose."

"What kind of procedure?"

"The kind a battlefield surgeon might use when performing emergency surgery." Holmes's eyes never left my face. "The kind of techniques you learned in Afghanistan."

The accusation bothered me. I thought of Blake again, a giant of a man who had been our anchor in the chaos of war, his laugh ringing across the compound even on the worst days. Blake, whose hands could thread a needle and crush a man, had appeared at my side, with impossible requests fulfilled, saying, "Doc, the lads need you focused on the cutting. Leave the finding to me." Blake, whose right shoulder had been laid open by an Afghan sword stroke.

"I would never—" I began, but Holmes cut me off with a gesture of his hand.

"I'm not accusing you, Watson. I'm trying to understand what happened. But to do that, I need you to be completely honest with me. Is there anything—anything at all—you remember from last night?"

I closed my eyes and tried to reach into the darkness shrouding those lost hours. There were fragments, impressions more than memories, "I remember... movement," I said slowly. "Being taken somewhere. And there were others, not only Polly. Men, talking about... about how perfect this is."

"Watson," Holmes said gently, "I want you to go to bed and rest. Try to remember what you can, but don't force it. Sometimes the mind reveals secrets in its own time."

I stumbled up the stairs to my bedroom; my legs were unsteady beneath me. "Don't try to force it," Holmes had said, but my mind was already betraying me, dragging me back to the merciless desert where the sun hung overhead like a malevolent eye and every breath seared the lungs. I hadn't been this exhausted since those final days at Maiwand, when exhaustion and horror had blurred together into something else entirely.

I fell onto my bed without undressing, hoping sleep would grant me mercy. But even as consciousness faded, I heard Blake's voice calling across the compound, "Keep the lamps burning, Doc. We'll be back before you know it." They had been his last words to me as a whole man, spoken with his usual confidence despite the ominous reports filtering in from the forward positions.

Sleep came erratically, bringing with it the familiar parade of accusing faces. Blake's eyes found mine as they laid him on the makeshift operating table, filled with the quiet acceptance I had witnessed in countless other dying men. But he was supposed to be invincible. Blake was supposed to survive when others didn't.

I worked with desperation in the dream, probing for the source of hemorrhaging I couldn't stop, trying to repair damage beyond repair. His blood ran between my fingers, and with each passing moment, I felt his life slipping away. He died while I was searching for a miracle that didn't exist, his hand going limp in mine.

I jerked awake, my shirt clinging to my skin with sweat. The phantom smell of desert dust and gunpowder filled my nostrils. How long had I been asleep? The light outside my window suggested afternoon, and I heard Mrs. Hudson's voice drifting up from below.

"Nearly time for tea," she was saying. "I was preparing some sandwiches."

Tea. Regular, English tea. I rose from the bed unevenly and caught sight of my reflection in the dresser mirror. My shirt cuff was stained with something dark, something suspiciously like blood.

The stain brought back the phantom weight of Blake's body as they carried him away, four men bearing their burden with grim faces. But there had been another patient after Blake, hadn't there? Bailey, with his minor wound and grateful smile. The bullet extraction had been almost laughably simple in comparison—a small-caliber bullet lodged in the muscle of his upper chest, well away from any vital organs. I had used my bistoury, the curved blade parting flesh with practiced ease, and the bullet had come out cleanly.

I tore off my shirt and examined the stain more closely. It was indeed blood, a rusty brown. But I hadn't been close enough to Polly's body to get blood on my clothes, and I bore no fresh wounds accounting for the stains.

With growing horror, I moved to my dresser, seeking the one tangible link to my past that had sustained me through these gloomy days. Simon Bailey's bullet.

My coat pockets were.

I frantically searched through every drawer, every pocket, every corner of my room where it might have fallen. Nothing. The bullet had been Bailey's and was now mine, my talisman against the darkness of memory, had vanished as completely as my recollections of the previous night.

My overturned medical bag lay open on my bed, its contents scattered. The instruments were all there, but my bistoury, the same blade that had cut through flesh with surgical precision in countless operations, was not there. Other medical instruments were all present, but the blade— it was gone. Doubt crept into my mind. My head started to pound with every heartbeat. Voices began to scream at me. "Save me, doctor!"

My hands began to shake as I gathered the instruments. There was blood on some of the tools, but how? The blood was fresh enough to be tacky to touch, and its presence mocked every principle I had sworn to uphold. I don't recall taking my bag with me to Buck's Row. How did this happen? I carried them to the bathroom with trembling fingers. Hot water steamed from the tap as I began to scrub the evidence away.

"This can't be, this isn't occurring." I repeated it over and over.

Steam rose from the basin, clouding the mirror above the sink. And as I watched in mounting terror, words began to appear on the glass surface in front of me slowly—letters traced by an invisible hand in the condensation.

"Trim the tree," the message read.

I stared at the words, my mind reeling. I had no memory of writing them, no recollection of standing in front of this mirror and tracing those letters with my finger. Was I seeing all of this? I started to look around the room in a panic.

Terror seized me completely. The implications were too horrible to contemplate, but they pressed against my consciousness with inevitable force. Had I killed Polly Nichols? Had I taken my surgical skills—honed through years of saving lives in the crucible of war—and used them to end one instead?

I stumbled backward from the mirror, my breath coming in short gasps, and fled the bathroom as if the walls were closing in around me. The faces of the dead swirled before my eyes like accusing spirits, their voices shattered my mind: "Why didn't you save us? Why did you let us die?" And underneath it all, a new voice, more terrible than the rest: "Why did you kill me?"

"Doctor Watson!" Mrs. Hudson's voice cut through the chaos in my mind. "Are you quite all right, sir?"

I put my hand against the door to stop her from coming in. I closed my eyes and tried to steady my breathing. "I'm fine, Mrs. Hudson. Just... a bad dream."

I opened the door, and she appeared in the hallway, her face wrinkled with concern. "You've been having a lot of those lately, if you don't mind my saying so. Perhaps you should see someone about them." She paused, her expression growing troubled. "Mr. Holmes left early this morning. Said he had business at the morgue."

The morgue. Where Polly Nichols lay still, her throat cut, and her body mutilated by someone with surgical skill. Someone like me.

I had to know the truth. I had to confront the one man who might have answers to the questions tearing my sanity apart.

I dressed quickly and left the flat, my footsteps pounding on the stairwell like the rhythm of machinery. The afternoon air was crisp and clean, a stark contrast to the suffocating atmosphere of guilt and confusion filling my rooms. I hailed the first cab I saw; my voice was rough with urgency.

"Blackheath Hospital," I told the driver. "And spare the horses for no one."

The journey to Blackheath passed in a blur of London streets and mounting dread. My reality was coming apart; dreams and flash-backs were combining, reminding me of distant gunfire and the sound of men dying in the merciless heat of Afghanistan. Each mile brought me closer to my destination, and the weight of my suspicions grew heavier, leaving me with serious doubts about my own sanity.

Dr. Shepard was in his office when I arrived, seated behind his desk with the same calm composure he had shown during our previous meeting. But there was something different in his expression now—a watchfulness suggested he had been expecting my visit, perhaps even anticipating it with satisfaction.

"Dr. Watson," he said, rising from his chair with what appeared to be genuine concern. "You look terrible. Please, sit down."

I remained standing, my hands clenched into fists at my sides. The muffled hospital sounds mingled with phantom scents of jasmine and desert dust, creating a nauseating blend that made my head spin.

"I don't know what's happening to me," I said, the words tumbling out in a rush. "I can't remember anything from last night after leaving The Frying Pan. I found blood on my clothes, on my instruments. And there's a woman— dead."

"Slow down, Doctor Watson." Shepard interrupted gently, his voice carrying the same professional calm nurses had used in Maiwand when delivering news no one wanted to hear. "Tell me everything from the beginning."

Something in his tone—too calm, too understanding—set off alarm bells in my mind. This was the voice of a man who was not hearing anything surprising him, nothing challenged his presumptions. It was the voice of someone who had been expecting this conversation.

"You already know," I said, my voice dropping to a whisper. "You know what happened to Polly Nichols. You know why I can't remember!"

Shepard's expression didn't change, but I caught a flicker of something in his eyes—satisfaction, perhaps, or vindication. "I know you've been under tremendous strain," he said carefully. "The nightmares, the guilt over your war experiences, the pressure of your work with Mr. Holmes. It's not uncommon for a man in your position to lose track of time."

I stepped away from him and grabbed the back of a chair. "Lose track of time?" I laughed, but it sounded more like pain than amusement. "Is that what you call it when a woman ends up butchered in an alley? When a man's surgical instruments are found covered in blood?"

The office door opened, and Nurse Whitmore entered, her face a mask of professional concern, reminding me painfully of the medical staff who had moved through our field hospital with quiet competence, bringing comfort to men who would never see another sunrise.

"Dr. Watson," she said softly, "Dr. Shepard has been helping soldiers like you for years. Men who've seen too much, done too much in the service of their country. There's no shame in accepting the treatment you richly deserve."

I looked from one to the other, and something turned in my stomach. They were working together—had been working together all along. This wasn't a coincidence or a medical concern. This was a trap, and I had walked into it with the same blind trust that had once led me to follow orders without question in the desert hell of Afghanistan.

"What did you do to me?" I demanded, my voice rising. "What did you give me at The Frying Pan?"

"I think you should sit down, Watson. We have a great deal to discuss." Shepard said as he moved toward me and opened his hand toward the chair in front of me.

"I'll stand, thank you." I reached into my coat pocket, seeking the comfort of my service revolver, but found only empty space. When had I last seen the weapon? The memory was gone, lost among the fragments of the previous night.

"Why?" I whispered. "Why me?"

I felt the familiar darkness creeping in at the edges of my vision. The nightmare faces of Maiwand, the men who had died under my knife, the terrible decisions made in the name of survival.

"Let me help you." Shepard's voice came from far away, ringing across the years like Blake's final words. "You've come here for help, so let us help you. Or maybe you want to forget, as you've forgotten so many other things? The mind has a remarkable capacity for self-protection, Watson. It can bury memories so deeply they seem never to have existed at all."

The room was growing darker; my vision was blurring again. I could feel myself falling, spiraling down into the same black pit from the previous night. Behind me, I heard Nurse Whitmore's footsteps approaching, the soft sound of medical instruments being prepared.

"Sleep now, Watson," Shepard's voice followed me into the darkness. "When you wake, we'll have so much more to discuss."

The last thing I saw before consciousness fled was Nurse Whitmore approaching with a syringe in her hand, her face wearing the same expression of compassion.

Then there was nothing but darkness, and the whispered voices of the dead faces asking why I had failed to save them—or worse, why I had chosen not to.

CHAPTER 5

The Unquiet Morgue

The London Metropolitan morgue hid itself in the underbelly of the King's Royal Hospital, the white porcelain tiles reflecting the pale light in patterns reminiscent of bleached bones. I had walked these corridors countless times, yet today the familiar silence felt different—weighted with questions demanding answers Watson could not or would not provide.

I arrived an hour before my appointed meeting with Inspector Bradstreet, as was my custom. The unfiltered truth exposed itself best in solitude, before the heavy footsteps of bureaucracy trampled the delicate traces of evidence into futility. Dr. George B. Phillips, Police Surgeon for the Metropolitan Police's H Division, was already at work when I entered the examination room, his tall frame bent over the pale form of a once living spirit.

Phillips was a competent enough practitioner, though his soft hands spoke of a life unmarked by the rigorous demands shaping Watson's surgical skill. The faint aroma of Irish whiskey continually accompanied his morning coffee, suggesting a man who sought solace in vices—a weakness I could understand, if not subtly respect. His slight lisp and unremarkable features made him easy to overlook, perhaps why he had developed the habit of speaking his observations aloud, as if reassuring himself of his own importance.

"Ah, Mr. Holmes," he said without looking up from his work, his voice carrying the familiar speech impediment. "Pleasure to see you, though I confess these circumstances are dreadful."

I approached the examination table. Watson's absence felt like a lost limb in the room—he should have been here beside me, his medical expertise complementing my deductive methods. Instead, he lay in our rooms at Baker Street, his mind fractured by whatever terrors had unfolded in those lost hours.

"Indeed, Dr. Phillips. What can you tell me about our victim?"

Phillips unveiled the remainder of the body he was already working on and picked up a folder. "Polly Nichols, given Christian name Mary Ann Nichols. Forty-three years of age, discovered at approximately three-forty in the morning by a carman named Charles Cross in Buck's Row. The body remained warm, proving death occurred not long before discovery."

The woman who lay before us bore little resemblance to the vibrant, if desperate, creature who had shared drinks with Watson at The

Frying Pan. Death had leached the color from her weathered features, leaving behind the ashen pallor of London's forgotten souls. Five missing front teeth left a dark hollow where her smile should have been, while her brown eyes stared sightlessly at the gaslight above.

"Her throat has been cut from ear to ear," Phillips continued, his clinical tone unable to mask the slight tremor in his voice. "The incision extends back to the vertebral column—a single, deliberate stroke caused immediate unconsciousness and death within moments."

I leaned in closer with my magnifying glass, studying the wound with intensity. The cut was indeed precise, executed with confidence in anatomical knowledge and steady hands. Too steady for an ordinary criminal driven by passion or desperation.

"The blade?" I inquired, though I already knew the answer.

"Extremely sharp and thin—a surgeon's scalpel would fit the profile, though a shoemaker's knife might serve as well." Phillips paused, reaching for his own magnifying glass. "But there's more, Mr. Holmes. Much more."

He moved to expose the victim's torso, and I felt my breath catch despite years of witnessing humanity's capacity for violence. The abdomen had been opened, a long incision running from her upper pelvis to the sternum. Her bowels protruded through the wound in a disgusting display, while additional cuts marked the right side of the body in a strange pattern.

"All of this work was postmortem," Phillips noted, observing my reaction. "The lack of significant blood at the crime scene confirms it. She was already dead when these alterations were made."

The word hung in the air between us like an accusation. Alterations. As if the killer had been improving upon his work, refining his technique with the disciplined patience of a craftsman perfecting his art.

"Dr. Phillips," I said slowly, my mind already racing through the implications of physical evidence, "in your professional opinion, what manner of person could have inflicted these wounds?"

"Someone with considerable anatomical knowledge, Mr. Holmes. The precision of the cuts, the deliberate avoidance of certain organs while exposing others—this wasn't the work of a common criminal. This was done by someone who understood the human body intimately and knew where to make their entry points."

The unspoken truth settled over us. Phillips walked around the table toward me and said, "Let me ask you Mr. Holmes. How many had the steady hands and clinical detachment necessary to perform such work?"

I didn't answer him. Watson's face appeared in my mind—not as I had last seen him, broken and confused in our sitting room, but as he had been, his surgeon's hands working miracles in conditions that would have defeated lesser men. Those same hands, once devoted to saving life, were now deemed by Scotland Yard capable of taking one.

The sound of approaching footsteps announced Inspector Bradstreet's arrival. I straightened, arranging my features into the cloak of professional detachment forged through years of experience. But inside, my mind churned with possibilities too terrible to contemplate.

"Holmes!" Bradstreet's voice carried the forced cheerfulness of a man trying to lighten the mood in the presence of death. "Punctual as always, I see. What have you and the good doctor discovered?"

I gestured toward the examination table, where Polly Nichols lay exposed in all her tragic vulnerability. "The killer possessed medical knowledge, Inspector. The wounds were inflicted with surgical precision, revealing someone schooled in anatomy. But there is more here than simple butchery. The timing, the public location, the nature of the mutilation—it feels less like a crime of passion and more like a carefully crafted message. It is almost... a piece of political theater, designed to incite a specific reaction from the public and the press. We must ask what larger purpose this death was meant to serve and what motives were involved."

Bradstreet's expression darkened, and I saw in his eyes the very conclusion taking shape in my own mind. "Yes, well, this brings us to a delicate matter, Holmes. We must speak of Dr. Watson."

The words I had been dreading were now exposed. I had known this moment would come, had seen it approaching with the unavoidable certainty of a gathering thunderstorm. Yet hearing Watson's name spoken in the context of murder felt like a violation of everything I held sacred.

"Watson is at home, resting," I said carefully but sternly. "He's been through a difficult time."

"An ordeal, leaving him with no memory of several crucial hours, during this time, he was seen drinking with the victim." Bradstreet stepped forward, his official bearing emphasizing the gravity of his words. "I'm afraid we can no longer treat this as a simple case of temporary confusion, Holmes. Your friend has become our primary suspect."

Before I could respond, two constables entered the morgue, their timid steps adding to the oppressive atmosphere. The younger of the two, PC John Neil, possessed the eager demeanor of a recent academy graduate. At the same time, his companion, PC Mizen, carried himself with the weary competence of one long past the point of innocence of London's darker side.

"Tell Mr. Holmes what the witnesses reported," Bradstreet instructed, his tone leaving no room for equivocation.

PC Neil cleared his throat nervously. "Well, sir, we questioned the patrons at The Frying Pan, and they all remember Dr. Watson drinking with the deceased. Several noted she was... attentive to him, and they left the establishment together."

"The barkeep specifically mentioned, Dr. Watson appeared to need assistance when departing," PC Mizen added. "Said the woman—Polly—helped him to the door. This was around midnight."

Midnight. I calculated the timeline in my mind, factoring in the estimated time of death and Watson's unexplained return to Baker Street. Hours remained unaccounted for, hours where anything might have occurred.

"There's also the matter of the walking stick," Bradstreet continued relentlessly. "The handle was found near the crime scene, though we've yet to locate the bottom portion. It's been identified as belonging to Dr. Watson."

I nodded slowly, my mind already working through the implications. Watson's military walking stick, a memento of his service in Afghanistan, had been with him for years. Its presence at the crime scene was damning evidence, yet something about the discovery troubled me. Why only the handle? What had become of the rest of the cane? The break point showed it had been broken over something or someone.

"I understand your concerns, Inspector," I said finally. "But I hope you'll allow me some time to investigate further before taking any rash action. Watson has served his country with distinction, and his character—"

"His service isn't in question, Holmes," Bradstreet interrupted. "But the evidence is becoming difficult to ignore. A man with the necessary medical skills, seen with the victim, with no alibi for the time of death... You understand my position."

I understood all too well. The weight of circumstantial evidence was building. Yet something fundamental troubled me about the case—a conflict between the man I knew, and the crime committed.

"Give me forty-eight hours," I requested. "If I cannot provide satisfactory answers by then, I will personally deliver Watson to Scotland Yard for questioning."

Bradstreet studied my face for a long moment, perhaps reading the desperation I struggled to conceal. Finally, he nodded. "Forty-eight hours, Holmes. But if Dr. Watson attempts to flee London, I'll have him arrested."

As the police officials departed, leaving me alone with Dr. Phillips and the silent accusation of Polly Nichols' corpse, I felt the familiar thrill of a complex puzzle beginning to reveal its patterns. Yet this case carried personal stakes, transforming an intellectual pursuit into something far more perilous.

Watson was in trouble—terrible, perhaps insurmountable trouble. And somewhere in the labyrinth of evidence and circumstance lay either his salvation or his damnation.

Forty-eight hours to save Watson from the gallows—assuming, of course, salvation was even possible. The evidence against him continued to mount with each passing hour, yet my instincts rebelled against the obvious conclusion.

I had observed Watson in countless situations, had witnessed his reactions to violence, to suffering, to the moral complexities defined by our work together. The man who had risked his life for others, who had shown mercy to the wicked and compassion to the lost, could not have been capable of such calculated brutality.

Mrs. Hudson stopped me at the entrance to 221B, her usually composed features marked by obvious distress. "Oh, Mr. Holmes, thank goodness you've returned! Dr. Watson has gone off in such a state—I've never seen him so distraught."

"Gone off? Where has he gone, Mrs. Hudson?"

"I haven't the faintest idea, sir, but he was shouting something about Shepard knows—kept repeating it as he tore through his belongings. He acted absolutely wild, Mr. Holmes, like a man possessed."

Shepard. The name triggered immediate recognition—Dr. Shepard at Blackheath Hospital, the physician Watson had consulted regarding his investigation into Private Bailey. If Watson had gone there in his current state of mind, the consequences could be catastrophic.

I took the stairs three at a time, my heart sank as I surveyed the destruction. Every drawer had been emptied, every closet ransacked, clothing and personal effects scattered across the floor like the aftermath of a violent tornado. Whatever Watson had been seeking, he had pursued it with desperate intensity.

The bathroom told an even more disturbing story. Water ran from the overflowing basin and pooled on the floor. Watson's surgical instruments lay submerged like sleeping fish, their metal surfaces gleaming beneath the clear water. I lifted them one by one, conducting a careful inventory, confirming my worst fears.

The bistoury scalpel was missing.

The curved surgical blade —the same instrument that could have inflicted the precise wounds found on Polly Nichols —had vanished along with its owner. The implications were harsh, yet I forced myself to consider alternative explanations.

Perhaps Watson had taken the instrument for protection, fearing his fractured memories might expose him to danger. Or perhaps—and this thought chilled me more than any other—he had removed it as evidence, seeking to destroy the tool used in the commission of murder.

Among the scattered belongings, I discovered Simon Bailey's jacket, the garment tied to Watson's recent psychological decline. The fabric carried faint traces of Thames water and the metallic scent of dried blood—reminders of the case which had roused Watson's dormant trauma and set him upon the path to ruin.

Bailey. The name resonated through my consciousness, calling forth memories of Watson's fevered recollections. The young soldier whose death had affected Watson so profoundly, whose personal effects had somehow survived their journey from Afghanistan to London's murky waters. What connection might exist between Bailey's tragic end and the horror befallen Polly Nichols?

I examined the jacket, noting significant details. The cloth was military issue, while stains and wear patterns told the story of hard service in unforgiving conditions. Yet something about the garment troubled me—a discordance between its apparent age and the events Watson had described. The cut was for a man larger than Simon Bailey's body, though only slightly; the size discrepancy suggests a man who would have gained weight in service rather than lost it—loose ends and unanswered questions that needed to be found.

Time was slipping away like sand through my fingers. Watson had a head start, and in his current mental state, he might commit acts sealing his fate far past any hope of redemption. I had to reach him before he encountered Inspector Bradstreet's men—before he spoke words that could not be unsaid or performed deeds that could not be undone.

Blackheath Hospital, a fitting name for such a foreboding residence. The building exhaled the sorrows of the inhabitants, men whose bodies had returned from distant battlefields while their minds remained trapped in foreign hells. As I approached the entrance, I found myself wondering how many other veterans had wandered through these halls, seeking a peace that had forever eluded them, forever out of reach.

Dr. Shepard received me in his office with the composure of a man accustomed to handling delicate situations—his immediate availability to see me stood out. The office carried the faint fragrance of flowers of jasmine—Jasminum officinale, if I was not mistaken—a scent of Eastern service. A surprising smell for an institute of this nature. One that noted a mental connection among those lads returning from service.

"Mr. Holmes," Shepard said, rising from behind his desk with superficial concern. "It's an absolute pleasure to meet you finally. How may I be of assistance?"

"I'm searching for Dr. Watson," I replied, studying the physician's face for any telltale reactions. "I believe he may have come here seeking... consultation."

"I'm afraid I haven't seen Dr. Watson today," Shepard answered smoothly, though the dilated pupils in his eyes suggested otherwise. "I must say, his condition during our previous meeting gave me sincere cause for concern."

I moved to the window, seemingly to observe the courtyard below, where patients in various stages of recovery took their exercise in the afternoon sun. In reality, I was positioning myself to observe better Shepard's reactions to my questions in the reflection of the glass.

"His condition?" I prompted.

"The nightmares, the guilt over his war experiences, the persistent trauma so often affect men who have seen too much combat." Shepard's voice carried professional sympathy, yet beneath the surface I detected something else—an inappropriate satisfaction.

"Dr. Shepard," I said, turning to face him directly, "did you serve in Afghanistan yourself?"

"I was stationed in Kabul for several years, though I never had the opportunity to serve alongside Dr. Watson. His reputation preceded him, however—the stories of his surgical skill were legendary among the medical corps."

The admission confirmed what I had already suspected, yet it raised new questions about the connection between these two veterans of Britain's imperial conflicts. What were the odds Watson would randomly encounter another Afghanistan veteran during his current crisis? Coincidence was possible, but in my experience, coincidence often masked more deliberate designs.

"I notice the jasmine fragrance," I observed calmly. "A reminder of Eastern service?"

"Indeed. I find it... comforting." Shepard's smile held cryptic secrets. "The mind forms powerful associations between scent and memory, Mr. Holmes. Sometimes those connections can be quite useful in therapeutic contexts."

Before pursuing this intriguing line of inquiry, a knock at the door interrupted our conversation. A tall orderly entered, his presence somehow commanding despite his subordinate position.

"Your two o'clock appointment is ready, Doctor," the man announced, his eyes briefly meeting mine with an intensity to convey some unspoken message.

"Yes, thank you, Eddie. I'll be along directly."

As Shepard prepared to leave, I made a pivotal decision for the investigation. "Perhaps I might wait here, in case Dr. Watson arrives while you're with your patient?"

"Of course, Mr. Holmes. Please, make yourself comfortable."

The moment Shepard departed with his orderly, I began a systematic examination of the office. Years of investigative work had taught me men revealed their true natures through the objects they chose to surround themselves with, and Shepard's personal space held secrets that might prove vital to Watson's fate.

His desk contained the usual medical paraphernalia, but hidden beneath routine correspondence, I discovered documents indicating interests more than conventional psychiatric treatment. References to experimental techniques, mentions of chemical compounds to induce memory loss or compliant behavior, and notes on the psychological effects of trauma combined with pharmacological intervention. In a locked desk drawer, numerous shipping and receiving receipts of orders beyond a mere doctor's need or want.

I read descriptions and patient reports of procedures sounding less like medical treatment and more like systematic manipulation of the human mind. If Watson had fallen into the hands of someone conducting such experiments, his current condition might be the result of deliberate intervention rather than natural psychological breakdown.

A noise in the corridor interrupted my investigation, and I quickly restored the documents to their original positions. Footsteps approached—multiple sets, moving with purposeful urgency. I positioned myself near the window, affecting casual interest in the courtyard activities while straining to identify the approaching voices.

"—must be more careful," one voice cautioned.

"—he's becoming suspicious," another replied.

"—the Bradstreet fellow was asking questions"

The conversation faded as the speakers passed audible range, but I had heard enough to confirm my growing suspicions. Watson's condition was not entirely accidental, and my presence at the hospital had not gone unnoticed.

As I prepared to leave Shepard's office, a figure appeared in the courtyard below. A man in a red military tunic stood among the recovering patients. Even at this distance, something about his bearing was familiar.

The man faced me in Shepard's window, his gaze meeting mine across the intervening space. For a frozen moment in time, we regarded each other with mutual recognition. Then he raised one hand to his temple in a subtle salute before melting back into the crowd of patients.

I left the hospital with more questions than answers, but with growing certainty, Watson had become entangled in something far more complex than a simple case of psychological trauma. The threads of a greater conspiracy were beginning to reveal themselves, and at their center lay secrets powerful individuals would kill to protect.

The solution came to me as I approached the familiar chaos of London's East End. I struck the cab's roof sharply, calling for the driver to stop at the corner of Dorset Street. If official channels were closed to me, I would employ less conventional methods of investigation.

"Wiggins!" I called out as the cab pulled to a halt. Within moments, a scruffy boy of twelve years emerged from the shadows between two tenement buildings, his eyes already assessing the potential profit in our encounter.

"Mr. 'Olmes!" the boy exclaimed, his gap-toothed grin reflecting genuine pleasure at seeing me. "Got work for us, 'ave ya?"

"Indeed, I do, Wiggins. Gather the others—quickly now. I require your particular talents, and the matter is urgent."

Within minutes, half a dozen street children had materialized around my cab, their faces eager despite the hour. These were my Irregulars—London's forgotten army of orphans and outcasts who could move through the city's shadows like ghosts, seeing everything while remaining invisible themselves.

"Listen carefully," I began, my voice carrying the weight of desperation. "I need you to watch Blackheath Hospital—the big stone building south of the river. One of you must maintain observation at all times. Look for a gentleman of medium height with a slight limp. He may be brought unconscious or under restraint."

"That'd be Dr. Watson, wouldn't it, sir?" asked a girl of perhaps ten, her features sharp with intelligence.

"Yes, Sally. It would indeed be Dr. Watson." I pressed coins into eager hands, more than I would usually pay but far less than Watson's life was worth. "But there's more. I need to know about the staff—particularly a short, bald man named Dr. Shepard and a tall, thin man, an orderly named Eddie. Their routines, their habits, anyone who visits them."

"'Ow dangerous is this job, Mr. 'Olmes?" Wiggins asked, his street-wise caution serving him well.

"Potentially dangerous," I admitted. "If you're discovered, claim you're seeking work in the kitchens or laundry. Under no circumstances are you to attempt entry yourselves. Observation and listening only."

As the children dispersed into the London twilight like a flock of sparrows, I felt both relief and terror. Relief I had taken action, terror at what they might discover. In a short time, Inspector Bradstreet would expect answers I might not hold.

But somewhere in the forbidding hospital, the truth was to be uncovered. And if Watson was indeed trapped within those walls, my young army of irregulars might be his only hope of salvation.

The game had entered its most dangerous phase, and the stakes had never been higher.

CHAPTER 6

Among the Madmen of Blackheath

The relentless beating of the grandfather clock in my study measured time with mechanical indifference, each tick marking another moment stolen from Watson's dwindling hope of salvation. I had worn a path in the faded red Persian rug through my restless pacing, awaiting word from my young army of irregulars. The weight of desperation pressed upon my chest— what intelligence might they gather? What fragments of truth could be assembled from their observations? Watson's life hung in the balance of their findings, and with it, something fundamental to my own existence.

I had grown profoundly dependent upon Dr. John Watson's steady company. When we first shared lodgings, he struck me as ordinary—a conservative military man seeking quiet home life after the chaos of foreign service. I had little desire for a roommate, yet financial realities and the pressures of time had forced me to find other opportunities. Watson proved tolerant of my irregular habits and impulsive temperament, qualities recommending him above other failed companions.

Gradually, our professional partnership had evolved into something approaching genuine friendship. His methodical mind provided the necessary balance for my more abstract deductions, while his practical medical experience translated academic conclusions into actionable results. Mrs. Hudson had observed on numerous occasions that she found Watson's company considerably more agreeable than my own. I had always dismissed this sentiment as housekeeping prejudice, though I recognized the underlying truth. Watson possessed those social graces, making him available to common humanity in ways forever eluding my nature.

Now, as the clock continued its unavoidable count toward dawn, I confronted the possibility of losing the one individual whose companionship I valued above all others. The prospect filled me with a species of dread I had rarely experienced in my professional or personal career.

The sharp ring of the doorbell interrupted my brooding mood. Pushing aside the curtains and peering through the front window, I observed a cluster of my minions assembled on the pavement below, their upturned faces bright with intelligence to report. They waved urgently, and I descended the stairs with hurried speed.

"What news do you bring?" I demanded, throwing open the door with perhaps excessive force. "Speak quickly—every moment may prove crucial."

I ushered them into the hallway, where Mrs. Hudson emerged from her quarters, properly attired despite the late hour but surprised by our nighttime conference.

"Gracious heavens, Mr. Holmes! Whatever is the meaning of this commotion? And who are these children at such an hour?"

"Mrs. Hudson, if you would be so kind as to prepare refreshments for our young colleagues—sandwiches and perhaps some biscuits. They have been engaged in work of the utmost importance."

"Aye, and some proper tea as well," added one of the more petite boys with the casual familiarity of London's street-wise youth.

I guided them up the stairs and into my study, where they sought the warmth of the fire with the practiced efficiency of those for whom comfort was never guaranteed. The flames cast dancing shadows across their eager faces as they arranged themselves in a rough semi-circle before my chair.

"Now then," I said, settling into my customary position and steepling my fingers. "What intelligence have you gathered regarding the hospital and its inhabitants?"

Wiggins, the acknowledged leader of this particular group, stepped forward. "Well, Mr. 'Olmes, we kept watch on the hospital like you told us, but we didn't see 'ide nor 'air of Dr. Watson goin' in or comin' out."

"But we did see somethin' else," he continued, his eyes brightening with the thrill of discovery, "the tall bloke—Eddie, you called 'im—came rushin' out the back with a couple of heavy sacks. Right struggling with 'em, he was, could barely get 'em up on his cart."

I retrieved my pipe from the mantelpiece, my mind already racing through the implications. "Tell me more about these bags, Wiggins. How large were they? Could you discern anything about their contents?"

"Big as flour sacks, they were," Wiggins replied, gratefully accepting a sandwich from Mrs. Hudson's tray. "He 'andled 'em careful-like, but they was heavy enough to make him grunt and strain somethin' fierce."

"And where did he take them?" I prompted, striking a match and drawing the flame into my pipe.

"Down to Butler's Wharf, 'e did. Stopped right in front of warehouse number seventeen. Funny thing though—soon as 'e rang the bell, them doors opened quick as you please. Drove right inside, 'e did, and wasn't in there but a few minutes before 'e came out empty-handed."

The assembled children nodded in unanimous agreement as they consumed their impromptu meal, their testimony gaining credibility through their collective corroboration.

"Building seventeen," I repeated, smoke curling thoughtfully around my words. "You are absolutely certain of this detail?"

"As certain as we can be, sir. But there's more— we couldn't see inside, we did hear sounds from within. Muffled voices they were, as if someone were callin' out with their mouth covered or tied up like."

My pulse quickened at this news. "Could you determine the nature of these voices? Male or female? Their apparent distress or emotional state?"

"Definitely a man, Mr. 'Olmes, and speakin' like a right gentleman—educated, nuttin' like the speakin' of the docks. But there was real fear in it, the kinda fear coming from being trapped."

"Is there anything else—any detail, however seemingly insignificant, which might prove relevant to our investigation?"

Sally spoke up with matter-of-fact delivery. "We made inquiries among the shoremen 'bout the particular building, Mr. Holmes. They all spoke of it with unease and to stay away if we knew what was good for us."

"What manner of unease?"

"They claim many of the dead veterans found floating in the Thames all came from the same warehouse. The pattern is always the same: men enter alive, but only their corpses emerge to be discovered in the river."

The veterans, Bailey, and the systematic nature of their deaths are all connected to the warehouse having received Eddie's mysterious deliveries. The pattern was becoming clear, though full implications remained shrouded.

"Excellent work," I said, distributing coins among the eager hands with perhaps greater generosity than financial prudence might recommend. "Your intelligence has proven invaluable, and I shall require your continued services in the days ahead."

"Right you are, Mr. 'Olmes!" they chorused, though Wiggins lingered a moment longer.

"You be careful now, sir," the boy said with unexpected seriousness. "This place... it ain't natural, what goes on there. Got a bad feeling to it, like somethin' wicked's taken root."

As I escorted them to the door, I felt both relief at their discoveries and terror at their implications. The truth was beginning to reveal itself, but each revelation deepened Watson's peril rather than offering hope of rescue.

Returning to my study, I sought solace in the mathematical precision of musical composition. I took up my violin and began Vivaldi's Violin Concerto No. 4 in F minor, allowing the sweet progression of notes to calm my racing thoughts and impose order upon the chaos of evidence and supposition.

Building seventeen would reveal what secrets lay within those walls, and whether Watson's salvation or damnation awaited discovery.

The successful infiltration of the warehouse would require preparation and disguise. Sherlock Holmes would be recognized by trained sentries, particularly those with military backgrounds who might have encountered descriptions of my distinctive appearance. The solution lay in complete transformation—not merely the adoption of different clothing, but the assumption of an entirely different persona.

I selected elements from my extensive collection of disguises: the weathered features of a Thames laborer, the bent posture of a man broken by years of manual toil, the distinctive aroma of fish and dock work marking me as belonging to the invisible army of workers sustaining London's commercial empire. A gray beard, carefully applied, aged my features by decades, while rough clothing and the practiced shuffle of chronic fatigue completed the transformation.

By dawn, I had inserted myself among the genuine shoremen gathering each morning at Butler's Wharf, seeking day labor in the endless process of loading and unloading the ships bringing wealth to the Empire. The work was brutal, but it provided perfect cover for systematic observation of the warehouse holding such sinister fascination.

Through careful attention to the rhythms of activity around building seventeen, I began to discern patterns that spoke of military organization rather than commercial enterprise. Guards changed positions with clockwork precision every twenty minutes; their bearing and alertness showed professional training rather than casual employment. Their posture and movements carried the unmistakable stamp of military service—veterans, most likely, recruited from institutions like Blackheath Hospital.

By the noon respite, I had counted eight different individuals involved in exterior security alone, rotating in pairs. The interior complement remained unknown, but the scale of the operation suggested resources a single physician would not command.

Wagons arrived empty and departed bearing wooden crates marked with the stenciled image of a dead tree—a symbol whose significance remained cryptic but held meaning for the operation's organizers. Each departing vehicle carried armed escorts, and no two convoys followed the same route; it truly was a distribution network valuing secrecy.

However, the building itself presented significant challenges for covert entry. No accessible windows offered potential ingress, while ventilation grates remained frustratingly high without assistance. The roof might provide access, but the fifty-foot gap between buildings made the approach equally impractical.

What I required was a diversion, something that would draw the guards away from their posts long enough to permit entry. The solution came to me as I observed their behavior: these were military men, trained to respond to distress calls and possessed of the ingrained gallantry characterizing professional soldiers. A woman in apparent danger would command their immediate attention and temporarily abandon their duties.

For such a delicate operation, I required an assistant who was both trustworthy and capable of delivering a convincing performance under pressure. The choice was obvious, though the request would be unprecedented.

Mrs. Hudson was engaged in her customary kitchen duties when I entered through the rear door wearing my dock-worker's disguise.

Her startled exclamation and defensive posture testified to the effectiveness of my transformation.

"Great heavens!" she cried, pressing one hand to her chest. "What manner of ruffian?"

"Peace, Mrs. Hudson. It is I—Holmes. Do not be alarmed by my appearance."

"Mr. Holmes!" she gasped, studying my transformed features with obvious amazement. "You gave me such a fright! Whatever has possessed you to adopt such a dreadful disguise?"

"I require your assistance in locating Dr. Watson," I said, looking into her eyes with an intensity conveying the gravity of our situation. "You may well be our only hope of success."

Her expression shifted from surprise to determination with the admirable speed of a woman accustomed to unexpected demands. "What would you have me do?"

"I need you to scream, Mrs. Hudson. Scream as if your life depended upon it."

An hour later, we had positioned ourselves at the corner of Butler's Wharf, where the evening fog provided additional concealment for our clandestine operation. I carried a lantern whose flickering light would serve as Mrs. Hudson's signal to commence her performance, while I concealed myself behind a stack of cargo crates within twenty feet of the warehouse entrance.

"Remember," I whispered, catching her eye across the intervening distance, "you are a woman in genuine terror, fleeing from a pursuer unknown. The fear must be absolutely convincing."

"Leave it to me, Mr. Holmes," she replied with the grim determination of a veteran conspirator.

I raised the lantern and waved it in the agreed signal. Mrs. Hudson launched into a performance earning applause on any London stage.

"Help me! Oh, merciful heaven, they're chasing me!" she screamed, running past the two guards with every appearance of genuine terror. "Please, somebody help me!"

The guards watched her pass, but their discipline held them at their posts. Mrs. Hudson, demonstrating the improvisational skills making her such a valuable member of our household, glanced back and noted their immobility. Without hesitation, she screamed again and collapsed to the ground around the corner, her cries carrying convincing notes of injury and desperation.

This proved to be the catalyst breaking their military command. Honor and gallantry overcame duty as both men abandoned their posts to assist what appeared to be a woman in genuine distress. I seized the moment, emerging from concealment and covering the distance to the warehouse door with swift, silent steps. The entrance consisted of a large portal designed for wagon access, within which was set a smaller door proportioned for human passage. The latch yielded to gentle pressure, and I slipped inside, closing it carefully behind me.

The interior of the warehouse lay shrouded in darkness, relieved only by a few lanterns mounted on the far wall. As my eyes adjusted to the gloom, I began to perceive the outlines of the space —a cavernous chamber filled with shadows, concealing any number of secrets or dangers.

Voices reached me from beyond the wall I pressed myself against, speaking in tones carrying both familiarity and menace.

"You bled for them, you killed for them, you sacrificed years of your life in their service," the first voice declared with bitter emphasis. "And what reward did you receive for your devotion?"

A second voice joined the first: "Your blood and the blood you spilled has watered the tree of empire. Now comes the time for pruning— trimming and removal of corruption and decay."

A third voice contributed whispered replies, indistinguishable, accompanied by footsteps moving closer to my position. I pressed myself against the wall and made myself as small as possible, hoping the shadows would provide sufficient concealment.

The movement ceased short of my hiding place. I controlled my breathing, straining to detect any sign of their presence while remaining motionless as a statue. After an eternity, the footsteps resumed, moving away toward another section of the building, followed by the sound of a door closing.

I waited several seconds before risking movement, then crept forward like a cautious predator stalking dangerous prey. Around the corner, I discovered a larger chamber revealing the true horror of the operation.

Twelve beds were arranged in precise rows, each occupied by a man secured with leather restraints. The occupants appeared to be in various stages of drugged stupor, their eyes vacant and unresponsive. A phonograph in the corner played a continuous loop of the same eerie sentences, rhythmic chanting accompanied by hypnotic drumbeats, while the air carried the distinctive fragrance of jasmine I had detected in Dr. Shepard's office.

I moved carefully from bed to bed, examining each face in the hope of finding Watson among the victims. These were clearly more veterans from Blackheath Hospital, subjected to whatever experimental procedures Shepard and his associates had devised. The sight filled me with rage, but also with growing fear—if Watson was not among these prisoners, where might he be found?

As I reached the end of the row without discovering Watson, despair began to cloud my judgment. Had I miscalculated? Was he imprisoned elsewhere, or had some worse fate already befallen him?

The sound of the door handle turning froze me in place. I dove beneath the nearest bed as footsteps entered the chamber, moving with purpose among the restrained victims. The intruders conducted some brief business before departing again, leaving the door slightly ajar.

This presented an opportunity I could not afford to waste. I slipped from beneath the bed and crept toward the door, peering through the gap to observe a smaller adjacent room. It appeared to serve as an office or record-keeping space, furnished with tables, chairs, and filing cabinets.

But there, resting on the central table like an accusation, lay a leather-bound journal whose gold-leaf monogram I recognized: *J .H.W*.

Watson's journal—the repository of his most private thoughts and professional observations. Its presence here could only mean that Watson had been captured —or worse.

I entered the room and seized the journal. A ventilation grate in the upper wall offered a potential escape route. I stacked boxes to reach it, kicked the aged metal free, and squeezed through the opening despite the ten-foot drop to the alley below.

Within moments, I was racing through the narrow streets toward the nearest cab stand, clutching Watson's journal like a treasure.

The cab ride to Baker Street provided time for reflection, though my nerves remained as taut as my violin strings. The journal's soft leather felt like hope in my hands, as if it carried a trace of Watson's essence within its pages. This could be the key to understanding his disposition and where he might have gone.

Watson had developed the habit of maintaining detailed records of our cases, often embellishing them with literary flourishes before publication. But past these professional accounts lay more personal entries—introspective passages revealing the inner workings of a mind I had come to respect and value.

Watson's room had been torn up as though it had been searched, Mrs. Hudson had reported, but the thoroughness of the hunt was now suspect. Had Watson conducted it himself in his confused state, or had others been seeking this journal? The questions multiplied faster than answers.

Upon reading the final entry, I felt troubling concern:

31st of August 1888.

Polly Nichols has been pruned from the tree. Four hours remain lost to memory. The incessant screaming will not cease—horrible faces of death swim before my eyes, and I feel the warm blood upon my hands. The cold steel trembles in my grip as justice finds its mark. They deserve their fate, these parasites who prey upon the innocent. Bailey deserved better. Blake deserved better. Smith deserved better. They all deserved better, and they all shall have their due.

The handwriting was unmistakably Watson's, though the sentiment expressed was alien to the man I knew. This appeared to be a confession of the most damning sort, yet something in the phrasing troubled me. The reference to "pruning" copied the voices I had heard in the warehouse, while the mechanical quality of the prose suggested a mind operating under external influence.

As the coach drew near to Baker Street, I observed Inspector Bradstreet waiting on our front steps with two constables and Mrs. Hudson. The sight filled me with relief—Mrs. Hudson had returned safely, but also apprehension, for I recognized the posture of men bearing grave news.

I descended from the cab and removed my disguise, revealing my true identity to the assembled officials.

"Ah, excellent theatrics, Holmes," Bradstreet observed dryly. "Mrs. Hudson has informed us Dr. Watson is not currently in residence."

"Correct, Inspector," I replied, settling down onto the front step with the weariness of a man burned by the truth he could not forget.

"Then perhaps you can enlighten us as to his present whereabouts?"

"I fear I cannot provide such information at this moment," I admitted, though I endeavored to maintain a tone of confidence I did not feel.

CHAPTER 7

The Ghost of Polly

I strained to open my eyes and saw only darkness, faint blurry fragments, and the smell of jasmine again. I moved to get out of the bed I was lying in, but soon realized I was bound by my ankles and wrists. I shouted for help until I nearly lost my voice. However, I found no relief, and no assistance came. The darkness in the room revealed little save for one small beam of sunlight coming from a boarded-up window in the far corner. I knew then it was day, but what day, and where was I?

I struggled to remember Nurse Whitmore and Dr. Shepard—a handhold, a syringe, and then nothing until I awoke here in this cell. I listened for any sound, anything to possibly give away my position. But neigh, absolute silence. It was deafening to hear nothing but my heartbeat. My restraints were thick leather. There was a buckle I barely was able to touch with my middle finger, but could not do more. I tried shifting in the bed I was lying on, but it too must have been secured to the floor. I was an absolute prisoner—my only companion—the sweet, flowery jasmine smell.

Hours went by, or must have. I watched as the only entertainment was the moving beam of sunlight across the room. It was getting darker, nearly evening now. My captors surely must be on their way to check on me, to see if I was alive. Why else would they bind me so? If they wanted me dead, they would've done it in short work. I drifted in and out of sleep for brief periods.

"Help me, Doctor!" someone screamed as I jolted awake.

The voice came from somewhere beyond the walls of my prison, echoing with the same desperate urgency I had heard countless times in battle. But this was different; this voice carried something more than physical pain. It carried betrayal, broken trust, and the destruction of innocence.

"Doctor Watson!" The voice came again, closer now; it was coming from the corridor outside my room. Heavy footsteps approached, and I heard keys jangling against metal. The door opened with a groan, reminding me of the gates of hell swinging wide.

I looked up—higher than I expected—as the doorway filled with a shape that blotted out the light. As my eyes adjusted, I made out the features of a man I had seen before—the orderly from Blackheath Hospital and the Frying Pan. His face was gaunt, his eyes hollow, mixed with grief and rage.

"You're awake," he said, his voice carrying the rough edges of London's East End. "Good. We need to talk."

"Eddie?" I croaked, my throat dry.

"Good, you remember. I was hopin' you would." He declared as he came into the room and shut the door quietly behind him.

"Polly, what happened to Polly? Did you?"

"I twasn't me, Doc. But for sure it was meant to be you."

Fragments of memory flooded my mind—shadowy figures moving in the darkness, voices speaking in hushed tones about duty and sacrifice. The phantom weight of my bistoury in my hand, the sensation and pressure of flesh parting beneath its blade.

"What do you mean?" I asked, though I dreaded the answer.

Eddie moved to the restraints on my right wrist, his fingers working at the buckle. "I mean, Dr. Shepard and Nurse Whitmore have been using you, just as they used Polly. Same as they're using the veterans in this city."

The leather strap came loose, and feeling rushed back into my hand like fire. I flexed my fingers, trying to work out the stiffness while Eddie moved to my other wrist.

"Using me how?"

"They're involved in a plot, Doctor. Using the lads from the war, the ones who can't sleep, can't think straight. They give them drugs to make them forget, to make them compliant and easy to use. They hypnotize them and convince them to do horrible things. Then they use them for their dirty work."

My left hand came free, and I sat up slowly, my head spinning from the sudden movement. The jasmine scent was overwhelming now, bringing with it a flood of disjointed images—Polly's face, the weight of something in my pocket, the sound of my own voice saying words I couldn't remember.

"Why are you helping me?" I asked as Eddie worked on the restraints around my ankles.

"Because Polly didn't deserve what happened to her," he said, his voice thick with emotion. "And because, Doctor, you're another victim."

My legs came free, and I swung them over the side of the bed. The room spun around me, and I had to grip the mattress to keep from falling. Whatever they had given me remained slightly in my system, making my thoughts fuzzy and my movements unsteady.

"There's another girl," Eddie said, pressing something into my palm. "Annie Chapman. She worked with Polly, dealing drugs to the veterans. She's got information about who's behind all this."

I opened my hand and saw what he had given me—another small piece of paper with an address scrawled in pencil. "Dorset Street," I read aloud. He quickly moved his hand over my mouth with a single finger over his in a hushing pattern.

"There you'll find Annie," Eddie said. "You've got to get to her first. But be careful, Doctor. They're watching you. The coppers think you're the Whitechapel murderer. Holmes has been searching for you incessantly."

Holmes. My dear friend, my partner in countless adventures.

"Find Annie," he said, helping me struggle to stand. "You have to uncover the truth of it all before it's too late."

He brought me to the door and pushed me to the side of the wall. "But first you need to get out of here alive," he said, moving to the door. "This place is crawling with Shepard's people. They'll be checking on you soon."

I followed him, my legs unsteady beneath me. The corridor was dimly lit, filled with a smell that reminded me of the powder-house odor of battlefields, wet, damp, and musty.

"This way," Eddie whispered, leading me down a narrow hallway lined with more locked doors. Behind some of them, I heard muffled voices, the sound of men weeping or calling out in their sleep. More victims, I realized. More broken soldiers being used by Shepard for his twisted purposes.

We reached a stairwell, and Eddie gestured for me to follow him up. The steps were wooden and creaked under our weight, each sound seeming to echo through the building like gunshots. At the top, we emerged into what appeared to be a storage area filled with supplies and equipment.

"There's a service entrance through here," Eddie said, weaving between crates and shelves. "Leads out to the alley behind the warehouse."

We made our way across the room and found the door. The locks were on the ground, opened, and the chains lay next to them. He opened the door, and cool night air rushed in, carrying with it the familiar sounds and smells of London—freedom, but also danger.

Out there, the entire Metropolitan Police force was hunting for me, believing me to be a savage murderer.

"Remember," Eddie said as I stepped through the doorway, "Annie Chapman, Dorset Street. But be careful who you trust, Doctor. Shepard has people everywhere."

The door was already closing before I could thank him. I heard the sound of a bolt sliding home, and I was alone in the narrow alley behind the hospital. The night was cold; I was wearing only the thin hospital gown they had put me in. I needed clothes and to stay hidden.

The alley was filled with refuse and debris—perfect for my needs. I found an old brown coat, discarded, torn, and stained, but service-able. A pair of boots, too large but better than bare feet. A cap to hide my distinctive features. Within minutes, I had transformed myself from Dr. John Watson, loyalist and physician, into another vagrant wandering the streets of London.

As I walked, I noticed something troubling. Despite Eddie's warn-ings about staying hidden, I found myself retracing my steps, dou-bling back toward the warehouse. Some compulsion I couldn't name was drawing me back to the place of my captivity.

From the shadows across the street, I watched as Eddie emerged from the same service entrance I had used. But he wasn't alone. Dr. Shepard was with him, and Nurse Whitmore, their faces animated with satisfaction rather than concern.

But there was something else, something chilling me to the bone. In Shepard's hand was a small glass vial he gave to Eddie.

"Time for the next phase," Shepard said, and the three of them disappeared in different directions.

I waited until the voices and footsteps faded, then slipped out of the alley and into the maze of London's streets. The city at night was a different world—darker, more dangerous, filled with shadows and hidden threats. I felt it was hard to walk straight; I undoubtedly didn't have to do much acting as a bum or narcotic user.

I made my way through the twisting streets, staying in the shadows, avoiding the gas lamps and the occasional constable on patrol. Every loud sound made me freeze, every footstep behind me sent my heart racing. But slowly, carefully, I made my way toward the East End, back toward Bucks Row and Dorset Street and the answers I urgently desired.

The buildings grew shabbier as I moved deeper into Whitechapel, the streets narrower and more treacherous. This was the London most people pretended didn't exist—the world of the poor, the desperate, the forgotten. It was also the world where Polly Nichols had lived and died, and where Annie Chapman was hiding with secrets.

I found my way back to the largest public house on Bucks Row without difficulty—The Frying Pan. Seeing it brought back screams of darkness and horror, chilling feelings I could not honestly remember nor forget. The windows glowed with warm light and echoed with laughter and conversation. For a moment, I was tempted to go inside, to seek warmth and companionship among the patrons.

But caution held me back. Even from the street, I saw men who were out of place—too well-dressed, too alert, watching the pub's entrance with the practiced eyes of predators. Were they police, or part of something larger? My mind in a fog prevented me from delving further into the twisting web of truths.

I chose the most prudent path and settled into the shadows of a doorway across the street, pulling my ragged coat tighter around my shoulders. The wait was endless, punctuated by the occasional drunk stumbling out of the pub.

Hours passed before I finally saw her—a woman in her forties, worn down by the hard life of the streets but possessing a certain poise. She emerged from the pub. Others inside call out to her as "Annie-doll"; she waved goodbye, weaving slightly as she walked. This had to be Annie Chapman, the woman I was searching for.

I waited until she was well down the street before following, keeping to the shadows and maintaining a careful distance. She led me through a maze of narrow alleys and cramped passages, past tenements leaning against each other for support. Finally, she stopped at a building on Dorset Street.

I shyly approached her.

Annie Chapman was leaning over with one hand on the side entrance to the apartment building, a bottle clutched in her other hand. When she saw me, she tried to stand up, but the effort exhausted her.

"Are you Annie Chapman?" I asked softly.

"Who wants to know?" she said, her stern voice slurred but recognizable.

"I want to ask you about Polly. I need to know what happened," I said, moving closer to her. "Eddie Walker said you were working with Polly, and you know about the drugs."

Annie gave a low, humorless chuckle. "Eddie Walker? There's a name I ain't heard in a while. Course, he's got reasons to stay away from the likes of me."

"What do you mean?"

"I mean, Eddie's got his own business to tend to," Annie said, taking a long drink from her bottle. "Him and his fancy friends at the hospital."

"You mean Doctor Shepard?"

"Oh, I know all 'bout da good doctor," Annie said, her eyes focusing on me with surprising clarity. "Been buyin' his special medicines fer months now. Good stuff, too—keeps da nightmares away, makes ya forget 'tings ya don't wanna 'member. Everyone wants a piece of it."

"You've been dealing drugs to veterans with Polly?"

"Course I have," Annie said without shame. "Good money in it, and da lads need help. But it ain't 'bout da money."

She reached into her pocket and pulled out a few white tablets.

"This here's the real stuff," Annie continued. "Not da watered-down version they give to da reg'lars. Tis what they use when tey want someone ta do somethin' special."

"Special how?"

"Special like forgettin' ya ever had a conscience," Annie said, her voice growing harder. "Special like bein' able to cut a woman's throat 'n not 'member doin' it."

The implications of this drug were the needed evidence I've been looking for. Annie pushed herself up from her perch.

"I'm sayin' they've been usin' it on lots a people," Annie said. "Vet'rans, mostly. Men already broke by war, men who'll believe anythin' if it means the pain stops."

"Ya, you look like one of 'em." She pointed her finger at me with a twisted, devilish scowl. "Yer their type. I see war in yer eyes." She began to laugh.

Everything spun around me as her laughter boomed in my mind. I thought about the drink Polly gave me. Did she slip this drug into it? Was this the catalyst for my forgotten time? But I found blood on my clothes, on my instruments. I had memories—but were they memories at all?

"Yer like all the rest," Annie continued, her voice coming from a distance. "Takin' da easy way out, blamin' everyone else for yer problems. Ya tink you're better than me, but yer worse. Least I know what I am."

The street was starting to blur around the edges, and I felt something stirring in my chest. A rage I didn't recognize, a hunger for violence having nothing to do with who I thought I was.

"Yer all the same," she said, but now her voice carried a different tone—calculating, deliberate. "Ya act so entitled. Ya tink the world owes ya somethin' 'cause ya went to war. But you're weak. Yer lookin' fer 'cuses ta do what ya want ta do anyway."

The smell of jasmine came back again. Faintly though. I took a deep breath. Why was I smelling this? Where was it coming from? The jasmine scent was overwhelming now; it surrounded me, and my vision narrowed to focus on Annie's face. Part of me recognized what was happening—the same loss of control I had experienced with Polly during the lost night, the same dissolution of will leading to my lost hours.

But another part of me, a darker part, was whispering she deserved reckoning. She was a symptom of everything wrong with this city, a diseased branch needing to be cut away.

"You think you're helping people," I heard myself say, though my voice sounded strange to my own ears. "But you're another parasite, feeding off other people's misery."

Annie backed away from me, and fear crept into her eyes. "Nah hold on. I 's talkin', just—"

"Just poisoning minds," I continued, stepping closer. "Just helping them turn good men into monsters. You're as guilty as Shepard, as guilty as all of them."

My hand moved to my coat pocket, and I was shocked to find something there—the familiar feeling of cold steel, the bistoury. When had I picked it up? I couldn't remember, but the sense of it was comforting; it felt right somehow in my hand.

"The tree needs trimming," I said, the words coming from somewhere deep in my subconscious. "The diseased branches need to be cut away."

But the voice in my mind was growing stronger, more insistent. She was right about one thing—I'd been weak, broken. I didn't have to stay that way. I could be strong again, useful: trim the tree, take matters into my own hands, avenge Bailey and the others, put a stop to this right now. I stepped closer to her.

"No!" Annie screamed with desperation.

I drove my hand toward her shoulder and slammed her against the fence between the apartment buildings. The impact took the breath from her lungs, and she gasped for air. But even as I held her there, even as I felt the bistoury's weight in my hand, something deep inside me was fighting back.

This wasn't who I was or who I wanted to be. I was a healer, not a killer. I had taken an oath not to harm, and no amount of manipulation could change the fundamental truth of my being.

But the struggle was agony. The jasmine scent was overwhelming, and I felt myself losing the battle for control. My vision was blurring, and there were voices in my head—not my own voice, but others, whispering instructions, giving orders.

"Make her pay," they said. "Make her understand. Show her what happens to those who poison the innocent."

The bistoury in my hand was eager to do its work. And part of me, the part broken by war and loss and guilt, wanted to let it.

Through the haze of chemicals and implanted suggestions, I became aware of movement in the shadows. Two figures were watching from a distance—men I didn't recognize, but their presence filled me with dread.

"No!" I shouted, pressing my hands against my temples as intense pain shot through my skull. My vision blurred completely, and the last thing I smelled was the damnable jasmine scent growing stronger, pulling me down into darkness.

The darkness I felt in my mind brought me to a halt, and my knees buckled as I fell, falling into the void of hell itself. The world around me was fading, and I ran. I ran down the alley, and my vision closed in. I was running in my mind, but I couldn't feel my feet moving. I felt hands grab onto my shoulders and pull my jacket, and a man's voice quietly said, "Relax, Doc, we've got you."

CHAPTER 8

The Disappearing Doctor

B radstreet exchanged glances with his subordinates before kneeling beside me, his voice dropping to a more confidential register. "There's been another murder, Holmes. A woman named Annie Chapman was discovered on Hanbury Street. The wounds are identical to those inflicted upon Polly Nichols—surgical precision, anatomical knowledge, the same grotesque methodology."

He stood and straightened his hat with the deliberate movements of a man delivering an ultimatum. "The evidence against your friend has become overwhelming. Two murders, both requiring medical expertise."

The implication hung in the evening air like a death sentence. Another victim meant another demonstration of the killer's surgical skill, another link in the chain of evidence binding Watson to these horrible crimes. Time had become my enemy. The gallows stretched toward my friend with each passing hour.

The net was closing around us both, and I feared even my considerable abilities might prove insufficient to save the one man whose friendship I valued above all earthly considerations.

Bradstreet met my eyes again and said, "I'll ask you one final time: Where is Dr. John Watson?"

As I shifted my position on the steps, Mrs. Hudson declared, "He departed to consult with Dr. Shepard," with decisive clarity. Inspector Bradstreet's expression turned to her, his weathered brow honing with professional interest.

"Shepard?" he inquired, pivoting back to face me. "And who might this Dr. Shepard be?"

"The chief psychologist at Blackheath Hospital," I replied, rising from the front step with the deliberate movements of a man whose body had endured strain. I dropped my theatrical beard into my cap and brushed the dock-worker's grime from my clothing while stretching muscles protesting the evening's energies. "I have reason to believe he may be intimately involved in these crimes, possibly as the architect of a conspiracy far more extensive than mere murder."

Mrs. Hudson preceded us into the house, announcing her intention to prepare a meal. The remainder of our assembly shuffled up the steps to my study, where I collapsed into my chair with profound exhaustion.

"Enlighten me regarding this, Dr. Shepard and his connection to Dr. Watson," Bradstreet commanded. His two subordinates lingered near the doorway, uncertain whether to remain standing or seek seats, their hats clutched nervously behind their backs.

"Do sit, gentlemen," I said, noting their discomfort. "Your nervous orientation is highly annoying."

Mrs. Hudson entered bearing coffee and sandwiches, and after brief pleasantries, I proceeded to relate the essential details of my encounter with Dr. Shepard and the evening's reconnaissance at Warehouse Seventeen. I exercised discretion regarding certain discoveries—Watson's journal, for one. There existed no compelling reason to provide Scotland Yard with additional circumstantial evidence potentially further implicating my friend in these heinous crimes.

The police departed with instructions to investigate the warehouse, though I harbored little hope they would discover anything of significance. As the door closed behind them, I sank into sleep in my chair, overcome by exhaustion, rendering further activity impossible.

I awoke hours later to a fierce ache in my neck, providing confirmation I had achieved sufficient rest to return to the investigation. I consumed what remained of the abandoned sandwiches, followed by several gulps of the cold coffee. Time had become my adversary, and I required immediate consultation with Dr. Phillips at the morgue.

The September morning matched my mood as I navigated the familiar route to Phillips's domain. "She was butchered in nearly identical fashion to Polly," Phillips stated without preamble as I entered. "Victim's name is Annie Chapman. Discovered this morning at six o'clock by John Davis at 27 Hanbury Street."

I approached the table where the victim lay beneath a blood-stained sheet. Phillips drew back the covering with a practiced flip, revealing wounds speaking of surgical precision applied with homicidal intent. Two deep gashes severed the trachea, while the abdominal cavity had been opened with the same grotesque methodology employed upon Polly Nichols.

"What can you tell me regarding the weapon?" I inquired, retrieving my magnifying glass to examine the wound patterns more closely.

"Identical blade, I would venture," Phillips replied, though something in his tone suggested uncertainty. "Same depth, same angle of approach."

I bent closer to the corpse, noting details Phillips's less trained eye had missed. The pressure points of discoloration around the shoulders told a story of restraint applied by smaller hands. The momentum and angle required to inflict these wounds suggested a shorter assailant. At the same time, the absence of specific bruising patterns on the neck indicated a different method of subduing the victim.

"You say identical, Phillips, but observe these abrasions," I said, pointing to subtle markings along the victim's arms. "The force applied here was different, more desperate, less controlled. This suggests our killer faced greater resistance or perhaps employed an assistant to restrain the victim while the fatal wounds were inflicted."

Phillips examined the areas I indicated, his expression growing thoughtful. "You may be correct, Holmes. I confess I had not considered the possibility of multiple assailants. But it could be the work of one man, or she had them before the killing."

"Perhaps, but I am beginning to doubt it. What physical evidence? Any discoveries among her possessions?"

He returned to his desk and retrieved an envelope, pouring two pills onto the scarred wooden surface. "These were discovered in her coat pocket."

The pills possessed a crude, homemade appearance, roughly pressed white tablets speaking of amateur pharmaceutical endeavors. I lifted one specimen and examined it through my magnifying glass, noting the irregular shape and, more significantly, a distinctive marking on the reverse side.

"There appears to be a symbol here resembling a tree branch or root system," I observed. "Have you conducted chemical analysis?"

"Completed before your arrival. Reagent tests confirmed the presence of alkaloids—definitely opium-based, though the precise formulation remains unclear. The symbol troubles me, Holmes. It suggests an organization, a trademark of sorts, or brand."

This discovery provided another strand connecting the victims to the veterans' opium trade, the crates I observed at the warehouse, and by extension, to Dr. Shepard's activities at Blackheath Hospital. The pieces of the puzzle were beginning to align, though the complete picture remained frustratingly elusive.

"Police Constable Reid serves as the investigating officer," he said.

"Indeed. Where is he now?"

"He departed not ten minutes past but left word he wished to speak with you."

Phillips summoned Reid, who entered with the confident stride of an experienced investigator. Unlike many of his colleagues at Scotland Yard, Reid possessed the intelligence to recognize when expert consultation might prove valuable.

"What testimony have you gathered from witnesses?" I inquired without waiting.

"John Davis, who discovered the body, reported that a neighbor named Cadosch heard a woman cry 'No, no!' at approximately quarter past five this morning, followed by a loud impact against the fence separating the buildings. The timing proves significant, as it establishes a narrow window for the crime."

"What of the victim's recent activities?"

"She engaged in part-time dealing and prostitution throughout the district. Chronic alcoholic, fallen on hard times. Interestingly, she had been attempting to secure volunteer work at the veterans' hospital in Woolwich." Reid paused, consulting his notes. "Her flatmate, Mrs. Elizabeth Long, observed her in conversation with a man at half past five near the rear of the building. She described him as approximately forty years of age, somewhat taller than the victim, with a slight limp, dark hair, and an unkempt appearance. Brown felt hat, with a dirty brown overcoat."

The description matched Watson's typical attire with uncomfortable accuracy. Yet thousands of London men wore similar clothing, making such details, at best, circumstantial.

"How did Mrs. Long determine the precise time?" I asked.

"The church bells chimed the half-hour as she departed the building. She was quite certain of this detail. But her timing doesn't coincide with Mr. Cadosch."

"In this neighborhood of Whitechapel, hearing a woman cry 'no, no' is hardly unique." I reflected as I sat down in Phillips's desk chair. Reid flipped through his notebook and put the pencil to his mouth. The gears moved in his brain, and I wondered what he was summoning up.

"It would be risky to kill her at this early hour with so many people waking up and starting their day. But no one saw anything of the actual murder. No other witnesses or any other evidence have been found as of yet, Mr. Holmes. But we've got the boys out searching in all the common lodging houses to find any man matching the description."

"Well, such efforts certainly make me feel ever safer," I said bluntly as I got up and walked out of the decrepit room. The lack of intelligence and deductive reasoning was stifling and oppressive. The suspect description troubled me, but my conviction remained firm: these murders were the work of multiple perpetrators employing Watson's appearance and medical knowledge to ingrain suspicion.

The afternoon light was failing as I returned to Baker Street, where I discovered a note from Inspector Bradstreet awaiting my attention:

Warehouse Seventeen was thoroughly searched. Nothing was discovered beyond ordinary shipping materials. Investigation continues. Will keep you abreast.

The message confirmed my suspicions. Dr. Shepard had undoubtedly anticipated official scrutiny and most likely had our residence at Baker Street under surveillance, clearing the warehouse of incriminating evidence. The man possessed resources and organizational skills, indicating backing from powerful interests. A single hospital psychologist could not orchestrate such an elaborate conspiracy without significant support.

I climbed the stairs to my study, my mind racing through the implications of the day's discoveries. The opium pills, the systematic targeting of veterans, the manipulation of traumatized soldiers—all pointed toward a scheme of staggering cruelty. But what was the ultimate objective? Simple profit from drug sales proved insufficient to justify such elaborate plans.

At my desk, I unlocked the drawer and withdrew Watson's journal. I opened the volume and began reading with frantic intensity, searching for any detail that might illuminate the growing darkness.

The early entries revealed Watson's deteriorating mental state with clarity. His nightmares of Maiwand, his guilt over patients he could not save, his growing despair at London's moral decay—all painted a portrait of a man approaching psychological collapse. My own obliviousness to his suffering filled me with shame. How had I failed to recognize the signs of his distress?

The later entries proved even more disturbing:

5th of May 1888

The dreams come and go, but I've had them the past four nights. The same dream, nightmare of Maiwand, the shelling, the blood, the screams. I wake, soaked in sweat, and it takes me a minute to gather my thoughts to where I am. I wish it would go away.

23rd of May 1888

Mrs. Hudson has been quite kind recently and has taken to making my favorite hen dish. I know she thinks it will cheer me up and help take my mind off. But as much as I tell her, it does, it most assuredly does not. Holmes is hard at work with his India case, and it has brought back so many memories of the Jewel of the Empire. I spent so much time there, but I wish I could forget it. His constant asking and questioning of the area and its ceremonies, and people, has left me sullen and despondent.

2nd of June 1888

I've had word again from the hospital in Woolwich, Blackheath. They are searching for army doctors to help with their patients and veterans. I again turned them down, but I feel sad and guilty about it. I should help, but I am hesitant.

15th of June 1888

The jasmine fragrance has permeated the air near Baker Street these past evenings. Despite closing all windows, the scent lingers. It triggers memories of Afghanistan I had hoped to forget—the same sweet aroma saturating the field hospitals where I witnessed so much suffering and death.

9th of July 1888

The nightmares are back again, but this time they are more vivid than before. It's as if I'm reliving the events in Mai-wand and all the terrible things occurring there. Why am I having so much trouble? The guilt and shame of it all, the lost lives, the men I tried to save but couldn't—I don't know what to do. I doubt myself, and my lack of sleep is making my health ever worse.

12th of July 1888

There is so much filth in the city, the beggars, the drunks, the drug fiends. The lost children are running amok because their parents are absolute wretches. Why are we living like this? The rot of garbage and decay is ever-present in the air. The rain doesn't wash it away—it merely brings it together in a sickening soup. Things need to be changed. Something needs to be done.

25th of August 1888

Simon was found today. His body was in the Thames, another overdose, another lost soul. Holmes is dismissive, and so are the police. No one cares. Simon was a good lad and had a life ahead of him. Why would this happen in this world? I will find out for myself and put a stop to it.

26th of August 1888

Simon's tunic was for sale in a pawnshop, and a pretty girl dropped it off. It still smelled of death. But the bullet was saved at least. I'd given it to Simon after taking it out of him. The token of life and death all wrapped in one. His death will not go unpunished.

27th of August 1888

I visited Blackheath Hospital today. Nurse Martha Whit-more recognized me from Maiwand—she was the last kind face I remember from those terrible days. But something has changed in her, a darkness I see reflected in my own mirror. She introduced me to Dr. Shepard, who claims revolutionary success in treating battle fatigue. Most disturbing was his apparent knowledge of my nightmares and the gaps in my memory. Someone slipped me a paper upon departing—directions to find "Polly" in Buck's Row.

29th of August 1888

The jasmine has returned, and I cannot account for hours of my day. I find myself in unfamiliar locations with no memory of traveling there. The voices in my head grow stronger, urging me toward actions that fill me with horror. I resist, but the struggle becomes more difficult with each passing day.

The pattern was unmistakable. His dreams and his flashbacks were all causing him to break from his mental state. The lack of sleep and the continual sight of depravity only added to his psychosis.

But it begs to ponder whether Shepard had been systematically manipulating Watson's fragile mental state, using the jasmine scent and some form of chemical influence to create periods of amnesia and susceptibility. The references to "Polly" and Buck's Row established a direct connection to the first murder, while the missing time periods suggested Watson had been compelled to witness or participate in acts that he could not consciously remember.

I closed the journal and pressed my palms against my eyes, fighting back tears of rage and self-recrimination. While I pursued abstract intellectual challenges, my closest friend had been drowning in psychological torment. The guilt threatened to overwhelm me, but I forced myself to focus on the immediate crisis. Watson's life hung in the balance, and unnecessary human emotional sympathy would not save him.

The journal entries suggested a psychologically fragile break. If Shepard is behind this, then Watson's fundamental civility had resisted the conditioning, explaining why the conspirators had been forced to employ doubles or accomplices for the actual murders. They needed Watson as a scapegoat, not as a killer. But to what end?

The urgent clamor of the doorbell interrupted my brooding. I descended the stairs to find Wiggins standing on the threshold, his small chest heaving with exertion. He had traveled a great distance with urgent news; the boy's face was flushed with excitement and exhaustion.

"What news do you bring?" I demanded, ushering him into the hallway.

"Dr. Watson, Mr. 'Olmes," he gasped, accepting the chair I offered. "I seen him not more than an hour past."

"Where, Wiggins? Speak quickly—spare no detail!"

"Down by the docks, sir, near the warehouse we been watchin'. But
'e wasn't inside—was walkin' along the Thames path like a man in a
dream. Movin' real slow and strange-like, talkin' to himself."

I knelt beside the boy's chair, studying his expression for any sign of
uncertainty. "You are certain it was Dr. Watson?"

"Aye, sir. Recognized his walk and the brown coat he always wears.
But somethin' was wrong with him, Mr. 'Olmes. Kept stoppin' and
lookin' around like he didn't know where he was. Passed right by me
without seein' me, though I was standin' plain as day."

"In what direction was he traveling?"

"Toward Blackfriars Station, sir, but movin' like he 'ad no particular
destination in mind. Just wanderin', really. And there were a couple
of blokes followin' him at a distance."

I began pacing the narrow hallway, my mind racing through the
implications. Watson was alive but under some form of chemical
influence, rendering him semiconscious, or he had a total mental
break and was unaware of his actions. If Wiggins had observed him
an hour past, he might be in the vicinity of the station.

"Wiggins," I said, turning back to the boy with sudden urgency.
"There is something else, isn't there? I can see it in your expression."

The boy shifted uncomfortably, his eyes avoiding mine. "Well, sir...
there was blood on 'is coat. Fresh blood, by the look of it. And 'e
was carryin' somethin' in his right hand pocket—like it might be a
knife."

If Watson had been discovered with a weapon and bloodstained
clothing, the case against him would become insurmountable. Even

my influence with Scotland Yard could not overcome such damning evidence.

"How much blood, Wiggins? Describe exactly what you observed."

"Splattered across the front of his coat, sir, like someone had been cut nearby. Not a great deal, but enough to notice. And the knife..." He paused, gathering courage. "It was one of them medical knives, sir. Sharp and thin, like what's in his surgeon bag."

I sat on the steps, overwhelmed by the implications. Shepard had achieved his objective, and Watson had been transformed into the perfect scapegoat, discovered in a compromised state with physical evidence linking him to the murders. The psychological manipulation had been supplemented by deliberate staging designed to ensure his conviction.

"Did anyone else observe him?" I asked, though I dreaded the answer.

"Aye, sir. A couple of dock workers pointed 'im out to each other. One of 'em said somethin' about callin' the police, but I didn't stay to hear more."

Time was running out. Within hours, Scotland Yard would have Watson in custody, and the weight of evidence would prove overwhelming. I had to reach him before the authorities, but tracking a man in his condition through the labyrinth streets of London would require resources I did not possess.

"Wiggins," I said, rising with renewed determination. "Gather your compatriots. Every available member of your organization must be deployed to search for Dr. Watson. Begin at Blackfriar's Station and work outward in expanding circles. He may be confused and disoriented, but he is not dangerous—whatever evidence suggests to the contrary."

"Right you are, Mr. 'Olmes. But what if we find 'im? What should we do?"

"Do not approach him directly. Watson may not recognize you in his current state and could react unpredictably. Follow at a distance and send word to me at once. Under no circumstances should you allow him to fall into police custody."

As Wiggins departed on his mission, I returned to my study to gather the materials I would need for what promised to be the most challenging investigation of my career. Watson's life hung in the balance, and I had perhaps hours to unravel a conspiracy months in the making.

The net was closing around my friend, but I was determined to cut through the strands before it could claim him. Whatever the cost to myself, I would not allow Watson to become another victim of this monstrous scheme.

CHAPTER 9

Footsteps at the Docks

The Thames River docks sprawled before me like the arterial system of the Empire itself, pulsing with the constant flow of commerce sustaining our great metropolis. Ships and ferries arrived and departed with clocklike exactness, their holds erupting with the wealth of colonies, while absorbing the manufactured goods proclaiming Britain's industrial supremacy. Among London's five million souls—a population having transformed our city into the largest on Earth—I sought one man whose life hung by the thinnest of threads.

Wiggins and his street gang had tracked Watson through the narrow passages near Tower Bridge, their keen little eyes and nimble feet proving invaluable in navigating the treacherous currents of London's underworld. The group's latest intelligence suggested Watson had taken shelter near the Chamber Street Blackfriars Rail Station, though his condition remained disturbingly unclear. Every constable in the metropolitan area would soon be searching for a man matching his description, and time had become my most precious commodity.

My taxi carriage crested the hill overlooking the rail station, and I observed the familiar bustle of afternoon commerce. The sight of Wiggins waving frantically from a street corner filled me with both hope—his urgency suggested developments proving either salvation or catastrophe. I tapped the roof sharply and leaped from the still-moving transportation, my feet finding purchase on the cobblestones.

"What intelligence do you bring?" I demanded, striding toward the cluster of street urchins who had gathered at the corner like a council of war.

"He was in there, Mr. 'Olmes," Wiggins declared, his grimy finger indicating an alleyway between two imposing commercial buildings. The structures rose like monoliths of London's prosperity. "Went in some time past, but we ain't seen hide nor hair of him since."

I pressed a shilling into the boy's eager palm while studying the building's architecture with growing perplexity. "Position yourselves at the rear of the structure and await my signal. Under no circumstances should you approach without my explicit instruction."

The group scattered with the silent efficiency that made them invaluable allies, disappearing into the urban maze. I approached the building, my trained eye cataloguing every detail of the construction, purpose, and potential for concealment. The ground floor housed legitimate commercial enterprises, with their well-dressed clientele flowing in and out regularly. Yet the location struck me as fundamentally wrong for a man in Watson's compromised condition and appearance.

The contradiction gnawed at my mind as I circled the building, searching for the anomaly my instincts insisted must exist. Watson, in his current state of mental disarray, would instinctively seek shadows and solitude. The bustling commercial environment would terrify a man struggling with fragmented memories and chemical influence. He would not willingly expose himself to such scrutiny.

I entered through the main entrance, and the building's interior confirmed my suspicions—dozens of legitimate businesses operated on the upper floors, their employees and clients creating a constant stream of witnesses acknowledging a disheveled vagrant's look. The contradiction between Watson's need for concealment and his apparent presence in such a location pointed toward a more sinister explanation.

Following my instincts, I made my way to the building's rear section, where the polished façade gave way to the utilitarian reality of receiving docks and storage areas. The transformation was immediate and jarring—pristine marble floors surrendered to worn concrete, while the refined atmosphere of commerce dissolved into the harsh pragmatism of manual labor. The workers' attention focused on the endless stream of crates and cargo.

My appearance in their domain drew suspicious glances, my gentleman's attire marking me as out of place among the rough-hewn men earning their living through physical labor. I adopted the direct approach such environments demanded, retrieving my coin purse with deliberate flashiness.

"Have any of you gentlemen observed a vagrant in a brown coat passing through this area?" I inquired, allowing the weight of my purse to speak louder than my words.

The workers exchanged glances, speaking in hushed tones. In their world, information possessed value, and they had learned to assess the worth of what they might reveal. One man approached with the cautious movements of a negotiator, his features betraying nothing of his thoughts.

"No one matching such a description has been through here recently," he stated, his voice carrying the careful neutrality of a man accustomed to dangerous questions. He paused, studying my face with the intensity of experience. "Though you might try the door yonder," he added, indicating a doorway escaping my preliminary observation.

I thanked him with appropriate monetary consideration and approached the indicated door, my lock-picking instruments making short work of its simple mechanism. The entry opened to reveal a narrow staircase descending into darkness, a passage leading directly into hidden secrets and shadows.

The descent into the building's subterranean levels felt like a journey into the city's buried conscience. Each step took me further from the legitimate world of commerce above and deeper into the realm of clandestine activities thriving beneath London's respectable exterior. The distant sound of muffled voices drew me forward like a siren's call.

I moved carefully, my senses heightened by the knowledge my discovery would likely prove fatal. The voices resolved into distinct patterns as I approached—three men engaged in conversation, their familiarity with dangerous business heard in their tones. Two possessed the hoarse quality of chronic smokers, their words punctuated by the rasping breath of lungs damaged by years of tobacco abuse. The third voice carried the lighter timber of youth, though showing premature familiarity with violence.

Their discussion centered on timing, shipments, and what the youngest described as "a right ol' time ahead." These men spoke of human suffering with the detached professionalism of merchants discussing everyday commodity prices.

"I'll take the good Doctor out with me," the younger voice declared. "See to it, or they'll have all our heads." The oldest man bluntly stated as they headed up the stairs.

I flattened myself against the cold stone, scarcely daring to draw breath, as two of the voices drifted upward. Their retreat came to my ears like a reprieve from death, though I was grimly aware that the one who remained was no less perilous than his departed comrades.

I maneuvered through the maze of crates and storage containers filling the underground chamber, my movements guided by years of experience in covert observation. Shadows danced in the weak light of a lone, scattered lantern, creating a hellish landscape designed to conceal unspeakable acts.

Through a gap between wooden containers, I observed the young man sliding open a heavy door invisible from my previous vantage point. The portal revealed another figure lying motionless on what appeared to be a crude bed or palette. My heart stopped as I recognized the familiar outline of Watson's brown coat and the distinctive silhouette of his form.

"My God," I whispered, the words escaping before I could contain them. "Is this truly him?" I thought.

The prone figure showed all the signs of heavy sedation, the complete lack of responsive movement, the unnatural stillness of limbs, and the absolute absence of conscious awareness. Watson had been reduced to a drugged shell, his brilliant mind clouded by whatever chemical compounds his captors had employed to render him compliant.

I watched in horror as the young man hauled Watson to his feet with the casual brutality of someone handling an inanimate object. My friend responded with the lifeless compliance of a marionette, his head rolling forward while his feet dragged uselessly across the floor. The sight filled me with a rage so pure and intense I nearly abandoned all pretense of stealth.

The captor, half-carried, half-dragged Watson toward another section of the chamber, their destination hidden from my view by the forest of storage containers before me. I began moving to follow them, my mind racing with plans for intervention, when a loud metallic bang resonated through the underground space. The sound was followed by the distinctive jingle of chains and pulleys—the unmistakable signature of a mechanical lifting device.

I rushed toward the source of the noise, my caution abandoned in the face of Watson's immediate peril. Another crash reverberated through the chamber, followed by the grinding of aged machinery under strain. By the time I reached the area where I had observed them, both Watson and his captor had vanished as completely as if they had never existed.

The wall before me presented an unbroken surface of aged wood and stone, showing no evidence of any mechanism or opening. Yet I knew with absolute certainty I had not imagined the scene I had witnessed. Watson had been here, drugged and helpless, and had been transported to some other location by means used for ulterior purposes.

I retrieved a used candle from a nearby ledge and coaxed it back to flickering life, its weak illumination revealing details daylight would have made obvious. The floor bore the unmistakable evidence of recent activity—footprints in various sizes, drag marks speaking of unconscious bodies being moved, and the accumulated trash of a space used for prolonged human habitation.

My investigation revealed the regular use of a hidden mechanism, as evidenced by a pattern of wear on the floor. The stone near one wall showed signs of repeated pressure, while the wooden panels bore the subtle scratches indicating frequent movement. I ran my fingers along every surface within reach, searching for the trigger revealing the chamber's secrets.

The candle's flame began to drain as the remaining wax approached exhaustion, casting increasingly frantic shadows across the walls. In desperation, I examined the floor more carefully, noting how the wear patterns seemed to focus on one particular area. Following my instincts, I pressed my boot against the indicated spot and was rewarded with the subtle snap of a hidden mechanism engaging it, followed by a loud "Click".

The wall pivoted inward with surprising smoothness, revealing a hidden chamber invisible moments before. The space contained the remnants of Watson's captivity: a simple bed, scattered personal effects, and the mechanical apparatus facilitating his disappearance. A crude lift mechanism dominated one wall, cables and pulleys disappearing into the darkness above.

The lift mechanism was gone, and there was no way for me to recall the contraption. Wherever the young lad took Watson, he was well away with him by now. Engaging in a chase would be fruitless. Hopefully, Wiggins and his fellow irregulars would see something more outside the building.

I examined the chamber. Every detail told a story of systematic imprisonment and psychological manipulation. Empty crates bore the distinctive stenciled image of a dead tree I had observed in connection with the trade at Blackheath. Food scraps and waste suggested prolonged occupancy by a single individual, while torn papers scattered across a makeshift table provided exciting glimpses of a larger conspiracy.

I gathered the scattered documents, my eyes scanning the shipping information and dates, painting a picture of methodical planning. Every delivery occurred at two-week intervals; all originated from the same source—Brookton Freight—and all bore the cryptic designation "Supply Item F." A single coordinating individual behind the operation, the receiving initials "E.W." appeared on every manifest.

This was not merely a criminal conspiracy but a systematic operation involving legitimate businesses and others unknown. The scale of the deception dwarfed anything I had previously encountered. At the same time, the methodical nature of the planning suggested resources and coordination that individual criminals could never achieve without significant help from higher sources.

My candle finally surrendered, plunging the chamber into absolute darkness. I felt my way back through the hidden door and into the main basement area, my mind tracing the facts from the implications of what I had discovered. Watson had been here, the evidence suggested, for days or weeks, subjected to whatever psychological and chemical manipulation his captors deemed necessary for their purposes.

Emerging from the shadowed depths of the building, I found my young compatriot Wiggins and his band awaiting me. A spark of hope lit their faces at my appearance, yet the gravity etched upon my own countenance must have swiftly dispelled it, for they read in my expression the somber import of what I had unearthed below.

"What news, Mr. 'Olmes?" Wiggins inquired, his young features furrowed with concern. "Did you find Dr. Watson?"

"He was here," I replied. "Did you note two men leaving?"

"We's been here the 'ole time, seen nothin' leavin' the dock." another lad blurted out. I distributed additional payment among the boys while providing them with revised instructions. "Maintain surveillance of this area and report any unusual activity. Dr. Watson may reappear, or you may observe other individuals connected to his disappearance. Your eyes and ears are now my most valuable assets in this investigation."

The boys dispersed with renewed purpose; their streetwise instincts ideally suited to the covert observation the situation demanded. I hailed a passing cab and directed the driver back to Baker Street, my mind already racing ahead to the next phase of my investigation.

The documents I had recovered pointed toward Brookton Freight as a central component of the conspiracy. The company's location at the corner of Cannon Street and Downgate Hill placed it at the heart of London's wealthy commercial district, while its ownership by Lord Reginald Barker suggested connections to the highest levels of political power.

Lord Barker's position as a prominent opponent of Prime Minister Salisbury's Conservative government added another layer of complexity to the conspiracy. His wealth and influence provided the resources necessary for an operation of this scope, while his political motivations offered a potential explanation for the systematic targeting of military veterans. The implications were staggering—if proven, they would reveal a conspiracy threatening the foundations of British Government and society.

The following morning, I found myself preparing for what promised to be a most dangerous reconnaissance. Lord Barker's prominence and political connections made direct investigation extremely hazardous, while his organization's professional competence suggested that any misstep would likely prove deadly. Before departing, I sent word to my brother Mycroft, requesting he investigate what he could about the government officials involved. Only his work could shed any real light on the happenings of the snakely world of government bureaucracy.

I selected the disguise of an elderly minister, a persona allowing me to move through respectable society while attracting minimal suspicion. The character required careful attention to detail—a slight stoop to suggest age, a simple walking stick for support, and the gentle demeanor of a man devoted to spiritual concerns.

Mrs. Hudson's startled exclamation as I descended the stairs confirmed the effectiveness of my transformation. "Good gracious!" she gasped, her hand flying to her chest in surprise.

"Do not be alarmed, Mrs. Hudson," I reassured her, though my voice carried the tremulous quality of advanced age. "I shall be absent until after tea, and there is no need to prepare breakfast. The Lord's work waits for no man. May God be with you!"

I departed through the rear entrance to avoid any surveillance that might have been established around our residence. The back streets of London provided excellent cover for clandestine movement, their maze-like complexity offering numerous opportunities for misdirection and concealment.

Brookton Freight occupied a corner building proclaiming Lord Barker's wealth and taste through every architectural detail. The high-quality brickwork and elegant proportions spoke of significant investment, while the gold-emblazoned crest above the entrance doors announced the company's prestigious connections. The polished brass handles gleamed with the attention to detail only a society high mark could maintain.

I established my observation post in a small café across the street, its window tables providing an excellent view of both the primary and side entrances to the building. The establishment's genteel atmosphere suited my priestly disguise perfectly, while the constant flow of customers provided ideal cover for extended surveillance.

The morning hours revealed a pattern of activity confirming my suspicions about the company's true nature. Legitimate freight operations occurred alongside activities with more clandestine purposes. The careful timing of certain deliveries, the discrete nature of some visitors, and the apparent security measures all pointed toward an organization conducting business far removed from normal commercial activities.

Two coaches arrived during my observation period, elevating my suspicions to near certainty. The first bore the distinctive "G" crest of our former Prime Minister, William Ewart Gladstone—a man whose liberal reform agenda had earned him the animosity of Queen Victoria and the current conservative organization. His presence at Lord Barker's facility suggested political maneuvers surpassing normal partisan disputes.

Gladstone's visit lasted more than an hour, during which I observed several individuals entering and leaving the building with obvious urgency. Their movements suggested the coordination of plans requiring careful timing. The associations were staggering—if Gladstone was involved in the conspiracy, it represented a threat to the British government.

The second significant visitor arrived in Lord Barker's personal coach, the royal crest recognizable to any observer familiar with London's political hierarchy. The vehicle's brief stop suggested the delivery of intelligence or instructions rather than a social call. A single individual emerged from the building to receive a folder of documents before the coach departed with evident haste.

The pattern of activity confirmed my growing suspicions about the true nature of the conspiracy I had uncovered. This was not merely a criminal enterprise but a political operation involving some of the most powerful figures in British society. The systematic targeting of military veterans, the psychological manipulation of damaged soldiers, and the elaborate framing of Watson all served a larger purpose, threatening the foundations of our democratic institutions.

As the noon bells chimed across London, I decided to try to observe the building's activities more closely. The lunch hour would provide excellent cover for reconnaissance, as the normal flow of employees and visitors would mask my presence among the crowd.

I positioned myself near the side entrance, adopting the demeanor of an elderly clergyman awaiting an appointment. The disguise served me well, as most passersby accorded me the respectful distance society maintained toward men of the cloth. My proximity to the building allowed me to overhear fragments of conversation providing crucial intelligence about the conspiracy's current activities.

A young man emerged from the side entrance engaged in urgent conversation with a superior, their words carrying the distinctive urgency of employees facing immediate deadlines. "The shipment for Blackheath Hospital must be delivered immediately," the older man declared, his tone allowing no argument. "Dr. Shepard's instructions were explicit—any delay could compromise the entire operation."

The younger man received a slip of paper with nervousness, his hands trembling as he studied the written instructions. His agitation created an opportunity I could not ignore. As he hurried from the building, I stepped directly into his path, creating the appearance of an accidental collision.

"Begging your pardon, Vicker," the lad gasped as our bodies collided. The impact sent his paperwork flying, providing the perfect opportunity for intelligence gathering. "I'm in a terrible rush and seem to have lost my delivery instructions."

"No trouble at all, my son," I replied, adopting the benevolent tone of a man accustomed to helping others. "Let me assist you in recovering your papers."

I gestured toward a nearby gutter while simultaneously palming the crucial document. The delivery slip confirmed my suspicions—"Delivery for Blackheath Hospital: Four crates of Supply Item F," exactly matching the pattern I had observed in the underground chamber. The connection between Brookton Freight, Dr. Shepard's hospital, and Watson's imprisonment was now undeniable.

"Here it is, I believe," I announced, producing the document with the satisfaction of a good deed performed. The young man accepted it with grateful relief before hurrying away on his urgent mission.

I hailed a passing cab and provided the driver with new instructions. "Blackheath Hospital, with all possible speed," I declared, settling into the seat while my mind raced through the allegations of my discoveries. The final confrontation with Dr. Shepard and his conspirators was approaching, and Watson's life hung in the balance.

CHAPTER 10

The Dead Tree

I dismissed the cab at a safe distance from Blackheath Hospital, preferring to make my final approach on foot through the narrow streets surrounding the facility. This conspiracy had me looking over my shoulder more than once. Just as I had Wiggins and the Baker Street Irregulars on investigative sightseeing, I had to deduce the same procedures were being taken concerning me as well.

Positioning myself in the narrow alley opposite the hospital's loading dock, I observed wooden crates and medical supplies moving in and out in a steady stream. A few fellow London inhabitants scurried off and dove into their sullen holes as I settled into my observation point, their presence a fitting commentary on the corruption festering within these walls. My walking stick served as both prop and weapon, the weighted head concealing modifications which might prove necessary in a possible confrontation ahead.

At precisely three o'clock, Dr. Shepard appeared in the courtyard like a general reviewing his troops. Nurse Whitmore accompanied him every step of the way. They approached the loading dock with a purposeful stride of individuals accustomed to absolute authority over life and death. I moved across the street to get a better look and to catch a phrase or two.

"Gentlemen, the operation is in full swing," Shepard announced, his voice carrying the bluntness of a surgeon. "The Southwark consignment departs at 1530 hours. The Whitehall consignment departs at 1545. There will be no deviation. Meet your contacts at the designated locations and relay the necessary goods to the party members."

The ten dock workers responded with the silent attention of veterans accustomed to orders. I recognized the psychological conditioning in their immediate compliance—these men had been systematically prepared for this moment through careful manipulation and chosen by Shepard for this project.

"The men are ready, Doctor," Nurse Whitmore confirmed, her tone equally devoid of warmth. "They understand the importance of the final push."

Shepard's gaze swept across the assembled group with calculating assessment. "See to it. This is only the beginning. It is a cleansing that is needed."

The ritualistic nature of his words were noted. "Cleansing," this was not merely political rhetoric, but the language used in his psychological manipulation and in systematic extermination. The parallels to military operations were deliberate—Shepard had transformed medical treatment into a form of psychological warfare.

"The time for pruning is nearly at hand," he declared, his voice rising with the fervor of a man convinced of his divine mission.

The assembled men responded in unison, their voices carrying the rehearsed precision of soldiers reciting an oath: "Trim the tree and burn the chaff!"

I shook my head as I recognized the conditioning mechanism at work. These words served as both a rallying cry and a psychological trigger, designed to override rational thought and replace it with a programmed response. The systematic nature of the indoctrination suggested months or years of work needed to assemble all the pieces.

Then, to my amazement, a familiar carriage rolled into the courtyard, bearing Gladstone's distinctive golden "G" crest. The former Prime Minister's involvement confirmed the conspiracy's political dimensions and linked him to Blackheath. The plot enjoyed support from the highest levels of government; his presence provided implicit endorsement of activities usually considered treasonous.

Shepard and Whitmore entered the Prime Minister's carriage, departing with the casual confidence of individuals certain of their ultimate success. Their absence left the courtyard in the hands of subordinates whose competence had been thoroughly tested.

Minutes later, a heavy wagon bearing the "Brookton Freight" designation rumbled into the courtyard. The nervous young man I had encountered earlier drove the vehicle, his hands shaking as he guided the horses into position. The connection between Lord Barker's freight operation and Shepard's hospital was now undeniably established.

The workers began unloading four large wooden crates, their movements undeterred by the containers' obvious weight. The crates were fashioned from cheap pine, yet their construction was sturdy enough to withstand handling. As the first container arrived at the loading dock, I noticed a detail that confirmed my worst suspicions.

Burned deep into the wood was the stark image of a dead tree, its roots exposed and gnarled as if ripped violently from the earth. The symbol matched those I had observed in the underground chamber where Watson had been held captive. This was the mark of the conspiracy—a sigil of death and uprooting serving as the perfect emblem for their revolutionary cause. "Trimming the dead tree indeed." I thought.

While the men continued unloading, my attention was drawn to a figure seated on a bench directly across the courtyard. The man was wrapped in a blanket. His pale eyes fixed on me with an intensity to penetrate my disguise.

I found myself compelled to approach this individual, whose presence in this location could hardly be coincidental. Crossing the courtyard with appropriate, disguised elderly caution, I positioned myself within conversational distance while maintaining the persona of a harmless clergyman.

"A chilly afternoon, my son," I began, allowing my voice to carry the gentle tremor of advanced age. "A trying day for old bones."

His response came slowly, as if each word required effort. "It's always cold now, Vicar," he replied, his voice carrying a gravelly whisper.

"You have the look of a soldier about you," I observed, adopting the gentle tone of pastoral concern. "Have you served Her Majesty?"

His answer revealed the systematic nature of Shepard's psychological manipulation. "We lost Kandahar, we lost Bombay... but we gained a ghost. We bled for them. Now the good doctor makes them bleed. The doctor with blood on his hands. We all do. But he made it art."

The "good doctor" could only be Watson. He had not been selected at random but was explicitly chosen because of his reputation among military veterans. His credibility within their community made him the perfect scapegoat for operations that required the appearance of a soldier-led rebellion.

"You're referring to Dr. Watson, I presume?" I pushed, my voice maintaining a priestly whisper. "Who chose him? What are you speaking of?"

"The ones who see," the veteran replied, his eyes regaining focus with disturbing intensity. "The ones who understand. Dr. Shepard. He showed us the truth. The politicians, the lords, they sent us to die for a line on a map. They broke us, and then they forgot us."

He then spoke in broken fragments of Watson with reverence, describing a moment during the retreat from Maiwand when the doctor had personally dragged him from the path of a cavalry charge. The memory carried genuine emotion—Watson had saved this man's life while under enemy fire, dressing his wounds even as rifle fire kicked up dust around them.

"He saved me," the veteran continued, his voice thick with gratitude. Then his expression hardened with frightening suddenness. "But the tree is sick. The rot is in the roots. The tree needs trimming."

I moved closer and sat beside him on the bench, recognizing the opportunity to gather crucial information. He took my hand in his, pressing it to his forehead with the desperate intensity of a man seeking religious absolution. "The work is not done. Your blood and the blood you spilled has watered the tree. Now it's time to trim the evil. Time to trim the tree. Forgive me Vicar."

The phrase again—these exact words had been spoken in the warehouse where the captives were held. The repetition was not merely slogans but carefully crafted psychological triggers designed to override thought and replace it with a programmed response or action.

Shepard had studied the work of Russian physiologist Ivan Pavlov, applying his conditioning techniques to human subjects. The repeated phrases, combined with pharmacological agents and sensory triggers like jasmine, created a system of behavioral control capable of transforming ordinary men into weapons of destruction.

"Have you had special treatments with Dr. Shepard?" I inquired, maintaining my gentle clerical manner.

"Shepard is a good man, a smart man. He's helping us, he's watching over us. Because they won't—they cast us aside and shun us," the veteran replied, his voice carrying the quality of a rehearsed response.

A nurse approached with an empty wheelchair, signaling the end of our conversation. I pressed for final intelligence before the opportunity vanished.

"What did they tell you to do, my son?"

"Trim the tree, burn the chaff, we spilled our blood," he replied, his words carrying the hollow resonance of systematic indoctrination.

The nurse helped him into the wheelchair, apologizing for the interruption and explaining it was time for the captain's therapy. As she wheeled him away, he began humming a low, tuneless melody, gradually resolving into "The British Grenadiers"—an old regimental hymn speaking of loyalty, battle, and unflinching advance.

The song served as a declaration of intent, a musical trigger reinforcing the psychological conditioning. Shepard had weaponized the patriotism, once making these men heroes, turning their loyalty into a tool for destroying the society they had once served.

I remained on the bench for a moment, allowing the associations of my discoveries to crystallize into actionable deductive reasoning. Watson's involvement was not coincidental but carefully orchestrated. His psychological vulnerability following his war service made him susceptible to the same conditioning techniques employed on the others. The conspiracy required a credible figurehead, and Watson's heroic reputation provided exactly the legitimacy they needed, but there is more to it.

The loading dock had emptied during my conversation with the captain, leaving the mysterious crates unguarded. This presented an opportunity that might not come again. I rose from the bench, resuming my persona of the confused elderly vicar who had taken a wrong turn.

The dock workers had gathered at the far end of the loading area, their attention focused on preparing the wagons for departure. The wagon master shouted instructions as two men quarreled over rigging procedures. Their distraction provided the perfect cover for closer investigation.

I shuffled toward the loading dock with apparent aimlessness, my head down and steps uncertain. The performance of elderly confusion rendered me effectively invisible to men focused on their urgent preparations. As I drew level with the marked crates, I feigned a stumble, lurching sideways and catching myself against one of the containers.

The maneuver provided precious seconds of contact with the cargo. My gloved fingers, trained in subtle manipulation, found the simple latch on the crate's lid. Final preparations were underway; the container had not yet been nailed shut.

With my body shielding my actions from observation, I lifted the lid slightly enough to glimpse the interior. What I saw confirmed my worst fears about the conspiracy's immediate objectives. The crate contained not medical supplies or provisions but instruments of systematic devastation.

The top layer consisted of dozens of crudely made torches; their heads wrapped in oil-soaked cloth. These were designed not for illumination but for arson on a massive scale. Below them lay stacks of placards bearing a stark message printed in block letters: "FEED THE FIRE." The slogan represented pure nihilism—a call to mindless destruction appealing to men whose reasoning had been systematically undermined.

At the bottom of the crate lay neatly folded piles of crimson fabric. Hundreds of red sashes had been prepared as uniforms, allowing conspirators to identify each other amid the chaos they intended to create. The simplicity of the system was its strength; no elaborate coordination would be required when the violence began, just a simple push, and the dominoes would all start to fall.

I heard the wagon master announce the final destinations, confirming the scope of the planned operation. "The first wagon to Southwark! The second to Whitehall!"

The targets were carefully chosen for maximum political impact. Southwark, the working-class district, was blamed for the uprising, while Whitehall, the government offices, were supposed to be destroyed in the supposed rebellion. The simultaneity of the attacks would create the impression of coordinated popular revolt.

I allowed the lid to fall back into place and continued my shuffling progress away from the loading dock. The urgency of the situation demanded immediate action—the wagons would depart within minutes, and once they reached their destinations, the conspiracy would be outside my power to prevent.

Hailing the first available cab, I abandoned my elderly persona in favor of direct command. "221B Baker Street!"

Mrs. Hudson waited at our door, her face etched with the worry accumulated during my absence. "A note arrived for you, Mr. Holmes," she announced, handing me an envelope bearing an official Scotland Yard seal. "It's from the Metropolitan Police."

The message within represented a masterpiece of bureaucratic manipulation. A full inquiry has been opened into the criminal activities and current whereabouts of Dr. John H. Watson. The investigation would be placed under the direct supervision of a consulting physician renowned for his work with military veterans—Dr. Elias Shepard.

I crumpled the note in my hand and threw it into the fire. The irony was devastating in its completeness. The conspiracy had not merely framed Watson for murder but had arranged to control the investigation, determining his fate. Shepard now possessed official authority to pursue Watson with the full resources of the Metropolitan Police, while simultaneously conducting the psychological operations driving my friend to his current desperate circumstances.

Before I could articulate my rage at this development, the door burst open with such force it crashed against the wall. My brother Mycroft stood on the landing, his large frame filling the doorway. All his customary composure had vanished—his cravat was askew, his face pale and slick with perspiration, and his eyes, usually so placid and analytical, were wide with desperate urgency.

"Sherlock," he gasped, leaning against the doorframe for support. "I was a fool. I was so occupied with Siam and the rumblings in India, I failed to see the weeds spreading in our own garden."

He staggered into the room, collapsing into an armchair with the exhaustion of a man who had been running for his life. "I received your message and began investigating Lord Barker and Minister Gladstone. The facts I've uncovered are clear. Prime Minister Salisbury's government is weaker than anyone realizes. Particular people have been put in place. There are factions, whispers of financial misdeeds."

"What exactly have you uncovered, Mycroft?" I said as I went to the table and poured myself a cup of tea. Mrs. Hudson brought a cup over to Mycroft. He pulled a folded paper from his waistcoat pocket, his hands trembling slightly as he smoothed it open. "The funding comes from three sources: Lord Barker's personal accounts, a discretionary fund controlled by Gladstone's liberal party faction, and most disturbingly, a series of anonymous transfers from overseas accounts. The conspiracy has colonial backing from many overseas companies."

I studied the figures he presented, my mind calculating the implications. "All these numbers, Mycroft—they are in unrelated areas. Perfect choices for moving and assembling what they need. But to what end do they have to be involved in this? Political tides change naturally over time. Why this type of conspiracy? What do they have to gain?" I said as I went to the mantel and took out my pipe.

Mycroft then pointed his finger in the air as if to summon God himself. "Stocks! Yes, by Jove, I would infer all the high-ranking members have shorted the stock market. If they did and the government was overturned, it would most certainly mean a market crash. They would all stand to make hundreds of thousands of pounds each. A King's ransom!"

The full scope of the deception became clear. The conspiracy was not merely planning to create chaos in government, but to ensure the chaos appeared to be the work of organized veteran revolutionaries rather than random violence. The distinction would be crucial in the political aftermath—random violence could be dismissed as

criminal activity, but organized revolution would demand a govern-
mental response justifying extraordinary means and tactics.

"What of the authorities?" I asked, though I suspected the answer
would provide little comfort.

"Inspector Bradford is aware of the threat but lacks the means to respond effectively. The Metropolitan Police can guard specific buildings, but they cannot prevent simultaneous attacks across multiple
districts in London properly. Moreover, Shepard's official involvement in the Watson investigation means the upper echelon of the
police force is under the control of this conspiracy group. Any police
action against the conspiracy could be interpreted as protecting a
suspected murderer."

"There is one additional complication," Mycroft added, his voice
dropping to a whisper. "My sources within the Cabinet suggest
certain members are aware of the conspiracy and may be allowing
it to proceed. The current government's public disapproval makes
them vulnerable to allegations of authoritarian overreach if they act
too forcefully against what appears to be a populist uprising."

I moved across the room and sat down next to my brother. "Gladstone and Lord Barker's involvement with other members of the
government itself proves their collusion in the conspiracy. The very
democratic institutions which should protect British society are
being used as weapons against it."

He gestured vaguely, as if encompassing the whole of London. "If it
succeeds, if they can create enough chaos to force the Queen's hand,
it will be the final straw. The government will shatter completely.
And she will call for a dissolution of Parliament."

Mycroft leaned forward, his eyes locking onto mine with terrifying intensity. "You must understand the scope of what we face. The empire is beginning to consume itself. This government will not survive the month."

CHAPTER 11

Catch the Ripper

"**M**r. Holmes, you must eat, please, for my sake, sir, eat something!" Mrs. Hudson pleaded with me. But I was too enthralled by this case and the spider's web in which we find ourselves. "The constables downstairs have eaten, and so should you," she stated directly as she walked away.

Bradstreet, in his characteristic manner, had stationed a pair of uniformed officers outside Baker Street, with the misguided hope that Watson might materialize or that I would lead them directly to him. Such thinking represented the pinnacle of investigative naivety—as if I would willingly deliver my most cherished friend and confidant into the hands of those who sought to destroy him. The notion was preposterous. Yet I found myself tormented by the mounting circumstantial evidence, which comprised this increasingly troubling case against my dear friend Watson.

Dr. Shepard now commanded the entire investigation with his purported credentials and psychological expertise. The irony was not lost on me. I found myself compelled to pursue this matter entirely without assistance, avoiding the interference of those incompetent lackeys at Scotland Yard and the Metropolitan Police.

Three weeks had elapsed since Watson's last confirmed sighting, and the trail grew progressively colder with each passing day. Every false lead, every case of mistaken identity reported by well-meaning citizens, consumed precious hours that might have been devoted to genuine investigation. The city teemed with rumors and phantom sightings, yet I remained no closer to locating my missing friend. The papers all had news of the murders, of the letters, and of the thousands of witnesses and sightings. Headlines screamed of terror in the streets. The Times devoted entire columns to theories and speculation. Even the penny press had abandoned its usual sensationalism in favor of breathless accounts selling papers by the thousands each morning.

Vigilante groups have been formed and are roaming the nights of Whitechapel and London's underbelly. Men who work honest jobs by day transform into self-appointed guardians after dark. They carry clubs and lanterns, moving in packs through the narrow streets. They have produced nothing more than harassment and bullying of anyone unfortunate enough to be out after sunset. Three innocent men have been beaten severely based on nothing more than a suspicious appearance or a foreign accent.

It was a press firestorm. Obviously, all are aimed at making money. They all have no real worry or care for the people—they enjoy the sounds of bags of coin dropped on their desks and care nothing to know how it may affect anyone published within their papers. Each edition outsells the last, each headline more sensational than its predecessor.

I crumpled them up and threw them into the fire. "NOTHING WORTH A THING!" I shouted. "Poppycock!" Once more, I put a match to my pipe and took long drags on the sweet tobacco as I dropped back into my chair. The familiar ritual provided small comfort, but my mind continued racing through the facts, searching for patterns in the chaos.

No, this is no time for idle chit-chat with the constables downstairs. We must find these people with whom Shepard and his group are engaged. Wiggins and his boys have seen nothing more. I had dispatched them to watch the docks with specific instructions to note any unusual cargo movements. The boys reported back this morning—the docks are clear of all suspicious transports, and the crates and box shipments have arrived at their intended destinations. But no word has been heard of them since. It's as if an order has been given to go underground and hide at all costs.

My only respite is Mycroft. He is working, I know, because he also has much to lose. His position within the government makes him uniquely vulnerable to the political ramifications of this conspiracy. His work investigating the government aspects of this case will undoubtedly bring success, but at what cost and when, I shall not endeavor to estimate. I must focus on my primary mission—the search for Watson and the identification of the real criminals.

I went to the window and peered below. Stationed as ever, those able gentlemen, the two bobbies. One leaned against the lampost, reading a newspaper. The other paced a small circuit, his boots clicking against the cobblestones in a rhythm which had become familiar over the past days. "Well, 'tis time to make our flight," I thought.

I went into my bedroom and threw open my closet. "What and who shall we be?" I pondered, then I had it—a chimney sweep. Yes, dirty, smelly, and no one you want to ask questions of or see much of. The disguise would allow me to move through the streets without attracting attention from either the constables or the growing number of vigilante groups.

As I was dressing, pulling on the soot-stained clothes and preparing the tools of the trade, Mrs. Hudson came down the hall and knocked loudly on my door. "Mr. Holmes! A carriage has arrived for you. There have been two more murders. Inspector Bradstreet is waiting for you in the carriage."

Alas, my escape has been canceled. I let out a deep sigh. "Be right there." I shed my disguise and put on my old skin. Murders plural. This shall be interesting. Indeed, it is tied to Watson in some way, no doubt. The real killer's pace was accelerating, pointing to either growing confidence or mounting desperation. I closed my door and headed down to the awaiting cab.

As we arrived at the crime scene, the crowds had already gathered to catch a view of the macabre. "The victims' names are Elizabeth

Stride and Catherine Eddowes. Both were murdered in the early morning hours. Victim number one was Stride, who was killed first." Bradstreet spoke as if reciting inventory rather than tragedy.

"Her body was found at Dutfield's Yard next door to the International Working Men's Educational Club on Berner Street." The location was significant—a place where political meetings regularly took place, where working men gathered to discuss their grievances against the broken system.

"Spare me the preliminary details, Inspector. I require immediate examination of the evidence." I strode past Bradstreet with purposeful determination, noting the constables had established a cordon around the scene while simultaneously obliterating any trace evidence through their careless movement.

A single slash was visible upon her neck, roughly six inches long, and had cut her left carotid artery and clear through her trachea. The precision of the cut and height of the woman made the murderer of average male height and right-handed. Death would have been instantaneous, preventing any opportunity for the victim to summon assistance. No other signs of injury were present. Her clothing was untouched, showing no signs of distress or manipulation. There were no signs of bruising or defensive cuts. No, this person was attacked from behind and all at once. They never saw it coming.

Elizabeth Stride had the obvious signs of chronic alcoholism—red-purple nose and cheeks, sunken eye sockets, and bitten fingernails. I studied her face carefully. She was forty, no, forty-five years old. Her mouth was also missing front teeth, and she had the hands of someone who had worked hard labor. Her shape also suggested several pregnancies. Judging by the late hour and location, she was not currently a nurturing mother.

I bent down close to the pavement stone. She lay half on the sidewalk, half in the yard. There was some evidence of a scuffle—boot marks, only one clear impression, revealing only the work of one man. The killer had approached from behind, struck quickly, and departed.

"No one heard anything? No one in the club?" I asked Bradstreet.

"Nothing whatsoever. The body was discovered by Louis Diemschutz, a steward at the club, who entered the yard with his cart. The victim was warm when he found her; they tried to help her, thinking she was still alive."

"And you continue to maintain this killer is Watson? You possess absolute certainty regarding this identification?"

"All available evidence points to his involvement, Holmes. I find myself compelled to reach this conclusion despite any personal reluctance."

I examined the ground. No cigarette butts, no dropped items, nothing to suggest anything more. It had rained again, and any further evidence had been washed away or destroyed by the imperative local peacekeepers trampling about. The investigation was being compromised by the men tasked with conducting it.

"So, victim number two? Take me to her." I stated as our sinister group of sightseers continued our tour de morts.

"Catherine Eddowes. Found her in Mitre Square. He had more time with this one." Bradstreet's voice carried a note of disgust he couldn't quite suppress.

We walked the short distance between the two crime scenes. The proximity was significant—the killer had struck twice in the same general area within a short timeframe. This suggested either supreme confidence or the pressure of some urgent timeline.

"Throat cut deep and opened up her abdomen up to her breast." Bradstreet bent over and pulled the white, blood-stained sheet to the side of the body. "Flung her entrails around her neck in a heap," he said as he stood up and put his hand against his mouth. "Frightful thing."

I slowly bent down and kneeled next to her. It was savage brutality. Hate was here—this woman had suffered the anger for two now. Her ear was also almost cut off, and some organs had been cut severely. These wounds showed a hurried butcher, not the precise cuts as before. One kidney was missing. The mutilations are peculiarly fascinating; they go past the thrill of death and into something more twisted, I noted in my mind.

"No witnesses either, I presume?" I asked.

"No, nothing. Only a broken whiskey bottle remained next to her. She had the smell on her as well. Her pockets were full—full of everything she owned," Bradstreet said. "Robbery was obviously not the motive."

"No, pure hate resides here. Hate again for women of this type."

"This type?" Bradstreet said as he tipped his hat up.

"Yes, inspector, all the murder victims were alcoholic women, ladies of ill repute, all had been or were mothers, roughly all in the same age range, and all coming from or going to boarding houses. Women society would not miss, nor would pay attention to in the dead of night." I moved across the confines of the scene.

"The pattern was deliberate. These were not random killings but carefully selected targets. Someone was choosing victims who would generate maximum fear while minimizing official investigation. Women whose deaths would be sensationalized by the press but not deeply mourned by respectable society."

One of the officers stepped forward. "There were some reports of a man being seen running away, but they are sketchy at best, and none of the descriptions were the same, so we can't rely on them."

"I suppose Watson's description matches one of them, though, doesn't it, Inspector?" I said with a condescending tone.

"Well, not quite, Holmes. Not quite." He rebuffed.

"The same assailant killed these women. The distance between the two murders is minimal. Mrs. Eddowes was an opportunity kill, facing the full brunt of the killer's purpose." As I stated these facts, a mob was forming around us. They were angry and were shouting at the police to do something. They weren't wrong, but they were filled with hate and desperation.

The look on their faces showed the darkness of hopelessness and obscurity. They showed remorse not for the victims but for themselves and the fear they might be next. This was precisely the reaction someone wanted to justify terror by extraordinary measures.

"You ain't doin' nothin' 'cause 'em ladies are nothin' to you!" they shouted from the crowd. Then I heard it like a shot. "Trim the tree!" A voice came from somewhere in the mob.

But this voice wasn't of the neighborhood. This voice was educated and well-bred. The words were spoken with diction and clarity, marking the speaker as someone with the means of an education. I pushed myself through the crowd to find the source. No one I saw fit the part—more and more commoners of the alleys had come to join in the mayhem, and a mass of humanity overran me.

I felt the grab of my shoulder as a constable pulled me back from the throngs and shoved me into a cab with Bradstreet, and took off.

We arrived at Scotland Yard as more angry citizens began descending on the building's exterior. The crowd was much like the last—angry, upset, and shouting for something to be done. Someone had painted "CATCH THE RIPPER" in red letters on the side wall of the building. The constables formed a line and allowed our cab to disembark safely on the steps.

As we followed inside, I glanced back and noticed a man across the street, standing in the shadows beside a closed shop. He was staring at the building—or was he staring at me? I was being pushed inside by the mob of people as I lost sight of him. I went to a side window, looking up and down the street to no avail. I could make nothing more of it; it was far too quick to get a better look, but I felt it a strange coincidence.

"Listen, this is getting out of control, and we need to put an end to this now!" shouted Chief Commissioner Anderson. He was a stout man, balding, wearing clothes far above his salary, and holding a cheap cigar in his right hand. His blustering was for show—the troops in the station thought him serious, but I saw through his charade. He was only doing what he thought he should, scared, yes, but totally clueless. A puppet being pulled by strings, and he may or may not know the identity of the puppet master.

I moved to the window to watch the growing crowd outside. "Yes, they're quite undone," I said with a slight smirk. "Most precarious. You really must do something, Inspector."

"Holmes, this is no time for games. Stop it." Bradstreet pulled me aside. "Take a look at these." He flopped down a folder with a stack of letters spilling onto the desk before us. "These—all of these—have been either received by the Yard, the Metropolitan Police, or local newspapers."

I sat down and began to inspect them closely. Looking at one, then flipping it over, smelling it, holding it to the light, then moving to the next. The handwriting varied wildly—some clearly the work of educated individuals, others barely literate scrawls. Most showed signs of deliberate deception, with writers attempting to disguise their natural hand. After a few minutes, I perused them all and kept one.

"This is the only genuine article in the lot," I said as I pushed the rest onto the floor. I slapped down a small letter with a note reading:

From hell

Mr Lusk, Sor I send you half the Kidne I took from one women prasarved it for you tother piece I fried and ate it was very nise. I may send you the bloody knif that took it out if you only wate a whil longer signed

Catch me when you can Mishter Lusk

"This letter, I assume, is addressed to Mr. Lusk of the local Whitechapel Vigilance Committee, and is the only one appearing authentic. The others are false, misleading, and most likely the work of newspapermen and attention-seekers. This, though, rings true. The mention of the kidney makes it unique—only someone with access to the crime scene would know this detail."

Bradstreet left and returned with another man, who handed him a small box. "This, Mr. Holmes, accompanied the letter." He placed the box on the desk and opened the lid. Inside was a glass jar that once held jam but now contained a piece of human kidney, preserved in what appeared to be wine spirits.

"Well, Mrs. Eddowes' kidney, I presume." I said bluntly.

"Dr. Phillips will provide definitive confirmation. We also expect his analysis to confirm the murder weapon remains consistent across all the related crimes."

"Indeed, I have no doubt Dr. Phillips will discover whatever facts prove most convenient for the current investigation."

I walked back over to the window, observing the growing crowd outside. They were writhing and seething with animosity, their anger palpable even through the glass. "They're extremely upset, aren't they? Curious why they would be. Murders happen nearly every day—they are no strangers to death. I wonder what's gotten into them so ferociously?"

"The papers are calling the murderer Jack the Ripper," Dr. Shepard said as he walked up to us. His sudden appearance in the room struck me as too convenient—he had a habit of materializing at crucial moments.

"Well, a name to put a face to, eh, Doctor?" I said as I stepped back from his arrogant presence.

"Yes, well, the paperboys sell what works, don't they?" He pointed to the crowd. "They buy it up, and they love a good mystery, don't they, Mr. Holmes? Too bad Dr. Watson isn't here to enjoy this case."

He moved to sit at the desk, and Bradstreet pulled the chair out for him. Shepard sat down and folded his hands over his walking cane's polished silver head, carved in the shape of a tree branch, the same symbol I had observed stenciled on the crates at Blackheath Hospital.

"Now that you're officially consulting on the case, I'm sure the murderer will be found. Your expertise as an alienist will surely provide the correct deductive reasoning, eh?"

I said and motioned to the constable next to me to open the door. "Time will tell, Mr. Holmes. And I'm sure Dr. Watson would agree with me. I'm sure he would agree with me on many things." He said with a sinister grin, confirming my suspicions about his proper role in recent events.

I'd heard enough. I walked out of Scotland Yard, angrier than the mob outside.

"Jack the Ripper," indeed, I thought as I walked away from the mass of people. "Truly putting a face to the name." No, I can't let Shepard provoke me—precisely what he wanted. I must focus on the larger picture.

If Shepard is now obliged to be at Scotland Yard consulting on the investigation, he cannot be directly involved in the hospital's daily operations in Blackheath. Someone else must be giving those orders—more members of this conspiracy are indeed needed to maintain operations across multiple locations. The plot requires coordination between the hospital, the government conspirators, and whatever group is carrying out the murders.

I walked along the streets of London, thinking, pondering, musing, and imagining what the ultimate goals were, what the final circumstances would be. The pieces were falling into place, but the complete picture remained frustratingly elusive. I found myself at the edge of Hyde Park, where I located a bench beneath a mature oak tree providing both comfort and concealment. This area of London housed the city's most affluent residents, individuals whose inherited wealth was evident in their clothing, transportation, and general demeanor. They moved through their daily routines with

complete ignorance of the social forces building beneath their priv-
ileged existence.

The contrast between their world and the increasingly desperate
circumstances of London's working classes was becoming more
pronounced by the day. Here, children played with expensive toys
while their governesses maintained careful supervision from nearby benches. Gentlemen in custom-tailored clothing and top hats
discussed business ventures and political developments as if recent
murders were occurring in a foreign country. Ladies in silk dresses
and parasols worried about the weather conditions affecting their
afternoon social tea.

In the streets and cramped tenements mere blocks away, women
were being systematically butchered while angry crowds demanded
action from authorities who were powerless to protect them. The
social fabric was being deliberately torn apart by forces that understood precisely how to exploit existing tensions. I sat back and closed
my eyes for a moment when I felt the tap of fingers on my shoulder.
I opened my eyes. A young lad of perhaps twelve years stood there,
a folded note in hand. I moved to take the note, but he dropped it
on the bench and ran off behind me, disappearing into the park's
winding paths.

I bent to retrieve the note. It was short and contained only a couple
of lines:

Holmes,

Stop looking for me. Find the Pruners.

J.H.W.

The handwriting appeared disguised—it was not original to Watson, but someone had gone to the effort to make it look like it was. The smudged ink showed it was written by a male right-handed, middle-aged person with some schooling, but not to Watson's level of education. The paper was thin and appeared to have been torn in half, as if it had been used once before for another purpose.

However, the scent was telling jasmine was present in the paper, along with sweet tobacco and turpentine. The same combination of odors I had detected at the underground chamber where the veterans were being held. I was being watched, followed, and observed by the plotters. "Stop looking for me," eh? Well, we shall not. But the Pruners" trim the tree"—trimming society, the crates bearing the tree symbol. This is all part of the same conspiracy.

I flipped the note over and saw a slight watermark in the paper when held to the light. It was partially cut off, but it left a clear impression of a capital letter "B" or possibly "E" —a clue to follow. The paper stock was expensive; it had come from a gentleman's stationery or a business office of some standing.

The message itself was a warning. Someone wanted me to stop pursuing Watson directly and instead focus on this group called the Pruners. Either way, the path forward was clear. The Pruners were the key to unraveling this entire conspiracy. Finding them would lead me not only to Watson but to the masterminds behind the reign of terror consuming London.

I rose from the bench and hailed a passing cab. There was work to be done, and time was running short. The next phase of their plan was already in motion, and I had to reach Watson before it was too late—for him, for London, and for the empire itself.

CHAPTER 12

Revelations

It was early morning when I received a note from Mycroft to come to the Diogenes Club post haste. The Club was his home away from home, and he did all his business there. I dressed quickly as I passed Mrs. Hudson on the landing, who was bringing up my breakfast. "No time now, Mrs. Hudson, I'm off to Mycroft," I shouted as I passed her, grabbing two pieces of toast along the way. As I walked outside, I stopped at the curb to hail a cab. But there, across the street, the same person in the shadows I had seen the day prior outside Scotland Yard. Our eyes met, and he ran around the corner. I followed at once; he had a lead on me, but I soon caught up to him, having a slight limp in his right leg.

I threw my cane between his legs at perfect timing, tripping him onto the ground. Onlookers gave me a sudden look of disgust, but I said plainly, "It's alright, nothing to see here," as I walked up slowly on the man.

He was roughly thirty years of age and had shabby brown hair with a slight scar across his forehead. He lifted his eyes to me, squinting against the sun behind my shoulder, holding up his hand to block the rays, with a scar on his right thumb and index finger. He was a soldier, or at least now a veteran. These scars were from repeated use of the Lee Enfield bolt-action rifle. The specific pattern of callusing on his trigger finger and his favored right shoulder confirmed extensive military training. I reached down to him with my hand open, offering to help him up.

He took it, went to one knee, then stood up, brushing himself off. "Some kind of trick, sir," he said. His accent told me of his upbringing in the far East End of London. "Mighty fine use of yer cane."

"Yes, well, I needed to get your attention, and I was not about to lose you in the alley."

"Watson sent me," he said directly, looking me in the eye. I knew he wasn't lying or trying to manipulate me. The directness of his gaze, the slight tremor in his voice—these were the signs of a man delivering a message of utmost importance.

"So, he's alive and well?"

"Alive, not well, but alive."

"Come with me." We took our leave and made our way once more to Baker Street.

Mrs. Hudson was out of sight in the kitchen when I called her. "We'd take the breakfast now, please." She shot me with a scowl. I smiled, and we proceeded upstairs. I motioned for him to sit at the table, which he took as Mrs. Hudson came in and set down the breakfast tray. I poured him a cup of coffee and one for myself. The man's hands shook slightly as he lifted the cup.

"Now, pray tell what your name is and what this is all about," I said as I sat back in the chair and templed my fingers under my chin.

"Name's Matthew R. Sloan. I'm private, or was, a vet from 'Gany. I'd been getting help 'n such down at Blackheath. We were getting better when Dr. Shepard arrived with nurse Whitmore. They was there to do a special treatment on us, got approval and such by the uppers. Well, it was suppose ta help with 'em nightmares and shaking we get every now 'n then. Strange it was, kinda funny and weird all at once."

"Strange how, funny how, please explain yourself completely," I demanded.

"Nurse Whitmore would give us a shot, and it would alter yer vision and seeing as such. Kinda blurry, but then it would make ya light-headed, like you felt you're fallin'. So we'd lay on a bed, they'd tie us down for our safety they say. Then we'd hear the same voice over and over, but I couldn't quite recall—it was like him reading."

"Him who, Dr. Shepard?"

"Maybe, but I knew he wasn't there, but his voice was." He paused, his eyes growing distant. "There was something about the voice... familiar like, but not quite right. Like hearing yer own voice when you're sick with fever."

The phonograph, expensive technology, the recording he had made, I thought. "Yes, go on."

"Well, we'd lay there for hours and then 'ventually we'd wake up and be in 'nother room, all sitting in chairs. But we weren't alone—there was a bunch of fellas, a group of us. Ed would come in and ask us about our mission."

"Ed, you mean Eddie, a tall, thin orderly?"

"Yes, sir, he's the one. He was a sergeant in the 66th Regiment of Foot in 'Gany, he served with some of the lads at Khyber Pass and Maiwand, we knew him. Made it easier to trust him, ya see. He'd talk about the old days, about how we'd been forgotten by them what sent us to fight."

"Did he mention a mission or operation?"

"I don't rightly know, I 'member some things about making them pay, cutting trees 'n such, about getting' our fair share. Something about showing them toffs what real men could do when they'd had enough."

"But nothing specific about the mission?"

"No, I only remember bits and pieces, time was in gaps ya see. I 'member some days and don't 'member others. I recall coming into the hospital but then I'd wake up in a warehouse. It was strange. The moment I saw Dr. Watson came then."

"Saw him where?"

"At the warehouse. He helped us wake up in the room. He was helping us with Nurse Whitmore. But..." He paused, rubbing his forehead. "But he was different. Sad like, but also... I don't know how to say it proper. Like he was there but not there, if ya take my meanin'."

"What did he say to you exactly?"

"He had the treatments too, but he was awfully sad, depressed like. He was troubled, his face pale and tired. I said to him, 'Hey doc, is this helping us really?' And he smiled and said we need to relax and let the medication work. But his smile... it weren't right. Like he was trying to convince himself as much as us."

"Was he giving you medication?"

"No, nurse Whitmore was, but he was like supervising her. Dr. Shepard came in then and he and him had a heated argument. Dr. Shepard didn't like somethin' and pushed Dr. Watson aside on his way out of the room. I heard him say something about 'not following the program' and Watson lookin' like he was goin' to be sick."

"When was this, what day man, can you remember?"

"Musta been a week ago. It was after Dr. Watson found me and gave me some different meds. He said it would help me faster, but I needed to go and make sure yer safe. He told me to follow ya, to watch out for ya. His hands were shakin' when he gave me the medicine, and he kept lookin' over his shoulder like he was afraid someone would catch him."

"No, no, quite alright. Did Watson say anything else? Do you remember anything else, anything about red sashes or pruners?"

"I helped load some boxes with red sashes in 'em, lots, like they were prepping an army, but don't know where they were going. 'Trim the tree' is all I remember. And there was talk about November, about Guy Fawkes Day, about showing them, what real revolution would be."

This confirmed all my suspicions—the grand plot, the psychological manipulation and conditioning, all the signs were there. But Watson helping Whitmore, I found it interesting and hard to believe. There must be more to this. But Shepard—I knew he was a liar. He knew where his murder suspect was. The problem was finding Watson before they could use him for their ulterior purposes.

Then I had an epiphany. The trigger—I wondered what Private Sloan would do if I introduced the smell of jasmine. I had been reading up on these methods Dr. Shepard had been utilizing. I got up and walked over to the fireplace mantle, took out a piece of dried jasmine, and brought it to him.

"Here, my young friend, smell this and tell me what you think."

He took a long look at it and sniffed a little. "Smells nice enough, like me mum's garden back home."

"No, Private Sloan, take it and smell it deeply, and close your eyes." I said with authority.

He obeyed as a good soldier would. He took a deep breath. Then he closed his eyes, and his head sat back in the chair. I stopped for a moment; he was perfectly still. His breathing became slow and regular, his face vacant of all expression.

"Private Sloan?"

"Yes, sir?" he said, his voice grumbled and devoid of personality. His face had turned blank as a slate, and his eyes as vacant. I decided to push further into his conditioning.

"Declare your mission and objectives."

"Mission is Operation Fawkes; objective is to bring light to the failure of our government and support of the people."

"What is your timeline, Private?"

"Operation will commence November 5th with a signal."

"What is the signal?"

"The fire will be lit."

"What fire?"

"The tree will be trimmed."

"Private Sloan, where is Dr. Watson?"

"I saw him last at Warehouse 13."

"Private Sloan, where is Warehouse 13?"

"Warehouse 13 is located in Lord Barker's Estate."

"Private Sloan, what will happen on November 5th?"

"The proletariat will rise. The riots will begin. The government will fall. The new order will take control."

"Who leads the new order?"

"Lord Barker. The tree will be trimmed of its rotten branches and roots."

"Awake, Private Sloan, awake and remember," I said, and I snapped my fingers.

Sloan popped his eyes open and faced me with a revelation. "I remember it all! How'd you do such a thing?" he said, his voice now trembling with the horror of understanding.

"It was all conditioning, my poor fellow. Conditioning and programming. They've manipulated you and your comrades into serving a revolution you never chose."

I called for Mrs. Hudson to bring him whatever else he needed. "I must go. You stay as long as you like—eat, rest, you are safe here."

Time was running out, and Mycroft was waiting.

The Diogenes Club had an impressive structure with its baroque charm. It was a four-story building nestled in the Pall Mall section of London's clubland, coincidentally in proximity between the Embassies of Japan, Germany, Russia, and the British Foreign Office. Mycroft's uniqueness was exemplified in the building, and its rules only allowed one to speak when invited. Silence was cherished above everything else.

As I arrived, the doorman was fully aware of my urgent communiqué and brought me straight up the grand staircase into Mycroft's private drawing room. The fire was so hot I felt as if I had entered a Turkish sauna; water was condensing and dripping down the windows.

"By Jove, Mycroft, it's hotter than Hades," I quipped as I went across the room to open the windows.

"No!" he shouted and ran to intercept me, pushing my hands down. "You can't—they'll hear us."

"Explain yourself, sir!" I demanded as I took off my coat and threw my top hat onto the desk.

"It's amazing, truly ingenious and diabolical." Mycroft was walking slow circles around the Persian rug in front of the fireplace, his hands wringing his fingers. "They've done it, and quite a good job. I see no way to stop it. The amount of planning and precision has taken months, if not years, to set this up."

"What have you uncovered? Speak, man."

I started walking beside my brother, hoping maybe his intellect and deductive reasoning would impart themselves to me. The sight of Mycroft in such distress was more alarming than any crime scene I had ever witnessed.

"Everything we thought and deduced will occur. There will be a coup d'état of the British Government. Selective heads of ministries have been coordinated to take control when the final match is lit. The Queen will have no choice but to order a dissolution of Parliament and a changeover. But this is only the beginning. Power is one part of this tangled web—control and money are the more important factors." He stopped abruptly. "And I'm guilty of encouraging and facilitating it." He nearly stumbled over to the chair and dropped into it.

"Guilty of what?" I asked, kneeling beside him.

"Guilty of ignorance, of pride, and of my own self-importance." Mycroft was no emotional soul—as long as I had known him as my older brother, he had been as steady and hard as iron, a character such as would have broken similar men. Seeing him like this, in this deprecating state, was astonishing.

"Start at the top, my dear fellow." I grabbed his hands and knelt beside him. "Tell me true, what is to come."

Mycroft lifted his weary eyes to me, red-rimmed and haunted. "The stock market. I didn't realize until it was too late. They approached me last year—a group of Lord Barker's financial advisors. They spoke of investment opportunities, of capitalizing on certain... market instabilities. Government bonds, shipping concerns, and manufacturing stocks. They said they had information about potential labor unrest, about economic shifts which would affect certain sectors."

He paused, his breathing labored. "I thought it was merely shrewd business, Sherlock. This kind of information flows through government channels every day. My principals were all invested. They brought me into their inner circle. So, I invested heavily—my own funds and money from my department's discretionary accounts. The returns were... substantial."

"How substantial?"

"Enough to make me wealthy beyond my current means. Enough to make me complicit." He stood and walked to the window, careful not to touch the glass. "But it wasn't until your note arrived to investigate that I realized the true nature of their work. They weren't predicting market instabilities—they were creating them."

"The murders, the riots, the social unrest—all of it designed to destabilize the government and crash specific sectors of the economy." I said and stood up.

"Precisely. And when the government falls, when Parliament is dissolved, when the Queen calls for new leadership... Lord Barker will be positioned perfectly. He has Gladstone's support, the backing of key financial interests, and the promise of restoring order to the chaos he himself created."

"And you'll profit handsomely from the collapse as well?"

"If I attempt to withdraw now, if I try to expose the conspiracy, I'll be revealing my own complicity. I'll be destroyed politically, financially, and personally. But if I remain silent..."

"You'll be an accessory to the overthrow of the British Government."

Mycroft nodded, his face ashen. "They've trapped me as surely as they've trapped those poor veterans. The only difference is I walked into their snare willingly, blinded by greed and ambition."

"I've uncovered more on the timeline," I whispered as I moved across the room and sat in his desk chair.

"November 5th. Guy Fawkes Day. The symbolism is deliberate—they're positioning themselves as the new Gunpowder Plot, but this time they intend to succeed. The riots will begin in Whitechapel, spread throughout the East End, and then engulf the entire city. The government will call for martial law, but the military leaders who should respond are either compromised or bought. In the chaos, Lord Barker will emerge as the only viable alternative as Prime Minister."

Mycroft withdrew from the window and approached the desk. "And Watson?"

"Watson is their unwitting catalyst. They've conditioned him to believe he's the Ripper, put him in place as their patsy. Orchestrated Watson as the killer of these lower-class women, in the most heinous and devilish way possible, to incite the masses."

I stood and began pacing the room. "We must find him before November 5th. We must break their conditioning and expose this plot."

"But how, Sherlock? If I reveal what I know, I'll be destroyed. If I remain silent, the empire falls. Either way, I'm ruined."

"Not necessarily, dear brother. There may be a way to save both you and the realm, but it will require courage, cunning, and no small amount of luck."

Mycroft regarded me with desperate hope. "What do you propose?"

"First, we need to reach Watson. Information has been uncovered regarding his location—Lord Barker's estate, warehouse 13. Second, we need to document everything—the financial transactions, the conspirators, the timeline. Third, we need to get this information to someone in government who hasn't been compromised."

"And fourth?"

"We need to stop Operation Fawkes before it begins."

"NO!" I screamed out loud and forcefully jarred my body. My eyes started to clear, and the haze surrounding me lifted like a blanket. I was riding in the back of a carriage at a swift pace. There were two other men with me, and I felt disoriented, confused, struggling to remember how we had arrived at this moment. The window of the door had bars. For a moment, I thought the Metropolitan Police had arrested me and we were on the way to jail. But these men next to me weren't constables. They wore red sashes.

The sight of those sashes troubled me, though I couldn't quite remember why. There was something significant about them, something I should know, but the knowledge remained frustratingly out of reach.

"Excuse me, but what is going on here. I demand answers," I shouted.

"Just pipe down and relax, Doc," the older of the two said. He rubbed his eyes and kicked the other man. "Eh, you with us?"

A groan of pain was his only response.

"What's wrong with him? Maybe I can help," I went to lean over and console him. My medical instincts were intact, even if my memories were fragmented.

The older man pushed me back into my seat. "Sit put, Doc. He's fine, just a little dreamy."

The carriage was traveling on a dirt road; there were no cobblestones, and I couldn't hear the usual bustle of city life. We were leaving London, heading into the countryside. But why? And more importantly, why couldn't I remember agreeing to this journey?

"Where are we heading?" I asked.

"We're takin' ya to Eddie."

The fragments of memory were like pieces of a shattered mirror, reflecting distorted images I couldn't quite bring into focus. But then it hit me—flashes of images, disjointed and terrifying. Screams rumbling in my mind. The hot, sticky sensation of blood on my hands. But whose blood? And why couldn't I remember the circumstances?

Polly, then Annie. Their names came to me in flashes, along with their screams. I put my hands up against my ears and closed my eyes, trying to block out the horrible sounds coming from inside my own head.

"There, there, Doc, you'll be right as rain in a bit," the older man said, his voice strangely soothing. He grabbed my arm and reached out to shake my hand. "My name's Kelly. Lieutenant Charles Edward Kelly. But you can call me Charlie. And this here little whip is Corporal Jimmy Haven."

He pointed to the younger lad next to him, who was now stirring slightly.

"We's pruners we is," he said as he tapped his red arm sash. "Been waitin' to meet you proper like. You're quite the important man, Doc. Quite important indeed."

"Pruners? What does it mean?"

"Means we trim the tree, Doc. Cut away the rotten branches so the good wood can grow strong. You remember, don't ya?"

Just as I was about to ask more questions, the carriage stopped, and the door was unlocked and opened. The two men filed out, and a woman's hand appeared through the door, beckoning me to follow. I got up and took the hand. It was Nurse Whitmore.

"Hello, Doctor Watson. I'm happy you made it," she said as she took me by the arm and led me toward the large estate house. Her grip was firm, almost possessive, and there was something in her eyes making me uncomfortable, though I couldn't say why.

We walked through the garden hedges, where many staff members were waiting for our arrival. Bags and boxes were unloaded from the carriage—supplies for what purpose, I wondered?

"Where am I and what happened to Annie?" I said, coming to a stop and looking her way.

"'Tis alright, Doctor, we have you now and we'll take care of you. You've had a right troubling time, and we aim to fix all of it for you." She pulled me along as we entered the grand estate.

It was an impressive structure. There must have been at least twenty rooms and a central gathering hall in the entrance to welcome guests far more distinguished than I. The opulence was overwhelming—crystal chandeliers, oak floors, paintings costing more than most people earned in a lifetime.

"And this is Lord Barker, our host," she said, turning slightly as she motioned toward an imposing man.

Lord Edwin Samuel James Barker, the ninth Duke of Avondale, walked into the room. He was tall and handsome, a gentleman whose looks spoke to his regal upbringing and whose poise was paramount. Everything about him radiated authority and confidence.

"Good afternoon, Doctor Watson. It is a pleasure to meet you finally. Welcome to my estate—I hope you find it comforting."

"Why, thank you," I said shyly, though something about his presence made me deeply uneasy.

"Nurse Whitmore, why don't you show our guest to his room and allow him time to settle in."

"Indeed, my Lord," she said with a slight curtsey as we proceeded to walk up the stairs.

When I turned, I saw Lord Barker accompanying my carriage companions to the door. There was something about the way he moved, the way he spoke, he was accustomed to being obeyed without question. This was a man who expected the world to bend to his will.

My head pounded, and I felt every heartbeat in my temples as we made our way up the stairs and down the hall to my room. The portraits lining the walls watched our progress—generations of Barkers looking down with expressions of arrogance and entitlement.

"Here is your room," Nurse Whitmore said. "And I'll be right next door. Why don't you lie down and try to relax, John."

"Did I do something... horrible?" I asked as she pushed me gently toward the bed.

"You need time to put things right, don't you, John?"

"Yes, I need to relax." I said as my eyelids became heavy. Time, this was what I needed—time to think, time to contemplate, and time to figure out what was happening to me. I knew I should flee, but I was exhausted and did not immediately feel in danger.

As I settled into the large, pillow-top bed, fragments of memory continued to surface. I was essential to these people somehow, central to their plans. But what plans? And why couldn't I remember agreeing to participate?

The last real memory was being in London, investigating the women who were taking advantage of vets like Simon. Then Eddie released me and told me to seek out Annie. But the time, the gaps, and the darkness. I pushed her and ran. Now I was here, in this grand estate, surrounded by people who knew more about my situation than I did.

I closed my eyes and tried to piece together fragments of memory, but they remained annoyingly obscure. Rest and hope for clarity to come with time was what I needed to concentrate on.

Outside my window, the sound of men training—marching feet, shouted commands, the clash of metal against metal. Whatever was happening here, it was bigger than my own confusion. Much bigger.

CHAPTER 13

Operation Fawkes

The howling wind rattled against the window of my lavish bedroom. Late October had come with the fierceness of a lioness. The red, yellow, and orange leaves fell across the manicured grounds of the Barker estate, where I had now resided for more than a week. Time moved strangely here—some hours stretched endlessly while others vanished without a trace, leaving me with fragments of memory refusing to form a coherent whole. Ghostly voices, screams, and, dare I say, hallucinations followed me here. I knew I wasn't insane, for the insane know not they are.

This particular morning, I was called to the grand dining room of Lord Barker. Standing on the center stage was a mahogany table that comfortably accommodated twenty. The room itself spoke of old money and power—crystal chandeliers cast prismatic light across oil portraits of stern-faced ancestors. At the same time, heavy velvet curtains blocked much of the natural light, creating an atmosphere of perpetual twilight and intrigue.

Three unfamiliar men to me occupied the far end of the table, their presence strikingly out of place in these posh English surroundings. The first man had a deep bronze complexion, as if he had spent considerable time under an unforgiving sun, though his hair—bleached nearly white by the same solar exposure—suggested extended service in India or perhaps Africa. His eyes held the wariness I had come to recognize in men who had witnessed too much of empire's darker workings.

Beside him sat a more brooding figure, weathered and aged by cold tundra far more than desert. Deep lines carved by wind and frost mapped his face, while his accent—when he occasionally spoke—carried the broad vowels of the northern Canadian territories. His hands, I noted, bore the calluses of a man accustomed to rough work despite his present comfortable circumstances.

The third member of this curious trinity possessed a tall, lean frame he carried with an almost jovial bearing, though his eyes betrayed a calculating intelligence perpetually at work. His demeanor suggested friendliness, yet I sensed something darker lurking beneath the surface—a secret none at this table wished to acknowledge or discuss.

My observations were interrupted by the entrance of both Lord Barker and a figure who took my breath away: former Prime Minister William Gladstone himself. The assembled company rose as one to honor these men of influence, waiting for the gesture that would permit us to resume our seats.

"Everything proceeds according to schedule," Lord Barker announced with confidence. "By this time next week, we shall find ourselves occupying the most advantageous position imaginable." His words carried the weight of absolute certainty, as if the future were merely another possession to be acquired.

"Indeed," Gladstone murmured, his voice barely above a whisper yet commanding complete attention. "However, we must execute this plan with precise care. There can be no margin for error, no room for improvisation. The timing must be exact, or all our planning will prove worthless."

The Canadian leaned forward slightly, his hands clasped before him. "My men will be positioned by this evening. They understand their roles completely."

"As do mine," added the sun-bleached gentleman with a slight nod toward his companions.

Then every eye fell upon me, as though expecting some contribution to this cryptic exchange—the weight of their collective gaze pressed upon me like a physical force. I cleared my throat nervously and raised my napkin to my lips, uncertain what response they expected.

"Dr. Watson," Lord Barker said, his voice carrying a note of satisfaction, "We have discovered the most perfect specimen for your next examination." He raised his hand in a subtle gesture, and one of the uniformed butlers materialized at his side. The other gentlemen rose from their seats and filed from the room without ceremony, leaving me alone with my host across the expanse of the polished table.

I remained seated, confusion evident in my expression. "I'm afraid I don't understand what you mean by 'specimen,' my lord. Are you referring to a medical case?"

Lord Barker's smile carried a quality making my skin crawl. "All will become clear momentarily, Doctor. Your expertise is precisely what we require."

The sound of approaching footsteps heightened my anxiety. When the double doors finally swung open, Nurse Whitmore entered with her characteristic briskness, though today she was not alone. Behind her walked a young woman of perhaps twenty years, her downcast eyes and hesitant movements hinting at either natural shyness or recent trauma. Her dress, while clean and properly fitted, bore the subtle signs of having been recently acquired—the fabric held the stiffness of new cloth, and the hem had been hastily adjusted.

Whitmore's firm hand guided the girl forward until she stood directly in front of my chair, as if presenting her for a blessing or approval. The young woman's hands shook slightly as she clasped them, and when she finally raised her eyes to meet mine, I saw a mixture of hope and terror that hit me to the core.

"This is Mary Jane Kelly," Lord Barker announced with ceremonial gravity. "She has expressed eagerness to make your acquaintance and would appreciate your professional assistance."

I studied the girl more carefully, my medical training automatically cataloging details. Her complexion suggested good health despite obvious recent stress. Her posture indicated education above her current circumstances, while her hands—soft and frail—spoke of a life not always requiring manual labor. Most disturbing, however, were the subtle signs of recent psychological manipulation I was beginning to recognize: the slightly dilated pupils, the way her eyes lost focus periodically, the manner in which she responded to Whitmore's touch with almost automatic compliance.

"I'm terribly sorry, but I must confess misunderstanding," I said, rising from my chair to address the young woman directly. "Miss Kelly, do you require medical attention? Are you experiencing symptoms concerning you?"

Before Mary Jane could respond, Lord Barker's voice cut through the air like a blade. "Why yes, Doctor, your attention is precisely what she requires." His grin widened, and I felt a chill having nothing to do with the October air seeping through the primeval windows. "Nurse Whitmore, please escort our guests to the examination room."

"Yes, my lord," Whitmore replied with a curtsey, managing to convey both deference and authority. She approached my chair with determined strides and grasped my arm with surprising strength. "Come, Doctor. We have important work to accomplish."

Nurse Whitmore's grip tightened as she led Mary Jane and myself through corridors stretching endlessly through the bowels of the estate. The young woman walked between us in silence. With each turn we took, the air grew heavier, more oppressive, carrying with it the unmistakable scent of jasmine—sticky and artificial, as if designed to mask something far less pleasing.

We descended a narrow staircase I had not previously encountered during my residence, emerging into what appeared to be a converted cellar chamber. The room had been transformed into a crude approximation of a medical facility, though one bearing no resemblance to any legitimate hospital I had ever witnessed. Surgical implements lay arranged upon a side table with theatrical precision, while three men I did not recognize stood waiting in the shadows.

"Here, Doctor," one of the men said, his voice carrying the cultured accent of education despite the sinister circumstances. He gestured toward the gleaming instruments with obvious satisfaction. "You'll find everything you require for your examination."

My medical instincts recoiled at the sight of tools arranged in this grim display. The scalpels were positioned with geometric exactness, the forceps aligned as if for inspection. Everything about this scene suggested preparation for a grotesque performance rather than legitimate medical practice.

"For what purpose?" I demanded, my voice betraying the growing alarm threatening to overwhelm my professional composure. "What precisely is the nature of this examination you speak of?"

The jasmine scent intensified as if someone had opened a vial of concentrated essence, and with it came something else—a voice sprang not from any of the present company but from the air itself. The words carried a hypnotic quality, making my vision blur and my thoughts scatter like leaves in the wind.

"John," the phantom voice whispered with terrible familiarity, "you have bled for them. You have sacrificed everything in service to their empire, yet they discarded you like a broken tool when your usefulness ended."

I stumbled backward, my hand reaching instinctively for something solid to anchor myself against the growing vertigo. "Who speaks? Show yourself!" I commanded, though my voice lacked the authority I intended to project.

"Doctor, there is no one else present," one of the shadowed men replied with obvious amusement. "Perhaps the strain of recent events has affected your perception more than you realize."

Whitmore approached, carrying a surgical gown she held open. "Here, John," she said, her voice adopting the same unnaturally soothing tone I had come to associate with the treatments at Blackheath Hospital and other warehouses. "You'll be far more comfortable in proper attire for your work."

"Work? Yes, work. Time to help those men."

"You know what to do, John. Time to work. Time to heal. Time to trim the tree."

Her words filled my mind. But why? I remember now helping others, sending Private Sloan to watch Holmes. But Shepard, he's always one step ahead.

The other men moved to assist, removing my jacket with movements that allowed no resistance, while the disembodied voice continued its insidious whispers. "You have sacrificed your health, your peace of mind, your sanity in defense of their interests. Yet when you returned broken and bleeding, they offered you nothing but empty promises and insufficient pensions."

My vision started to double, then tripled, as waves of nausea crashed over me with increasing intensity. The familiar headaches plaguing me since my return from Afghanistan intensified to a degree, making coherent thought nearly impossible. I reached for the instrument table to steady myself, and my fingers closed around the steel of a scalpel—the weight of it somehow reassuring in my trembling grip.

"John, you have bled for them," the voice repeated with hypnotic insistence. "Now it is time to make them bleed in return."

Through my compromised vision, I saw Whitmore approaching with a syringe ready for injection, her movements slow and deliberate. The jasmine scent had become so overwhelming I could taste it, while the phantom screams haunting my dreams since Maiwand reverberated through the chamber with renewed intensity.

"Stop this," I gasped, pressing my free hand against my forehead in a futile attempt to silence the screams in my skull. "Please, I beg you, make it stop."

"Relax, Dr. Watson," Whitmore crooned as she drew nearer. "Allow me to help you find the peace you've sought for so long."

Something deep within my military training, some survival instinct keeping me alive through countless engagements, asserted itself through the fog of manipulation. Before unconscious thought could intervene, I had spun around and seized Mary Jane Kelly, pressing the scalpel to her throat while positioning myself between her terrified body and the advancing nurse.

"Stand back," I commanded with an authority that surprised even me. "Release us, or I swear by everything holy, I will open this woman up."

Whitmore froze mid-step, her eyes widening with what might have been genuine surprise. The three men emerged from their shadowed positions, moving to encircle us.

"Back, I say!" I pressed the blade more firmly against Miss Kelly's neck, feeling her pulse racing beneath the sharp edge. "Allow us passage from this chamber, and I give you my word as a gentleman, no harm will befall her."

"But Doctor," Whitmore replied with mock concern, "she has volunteered for this procedure. Miss Kelly came here of her own free will, eager to assist in your important work."

"Yes," one of the men added with obvious satisfaction, "she understands the vital contribution she will make to your treatment."

I began backing toward the door we had entered, half-carrying the terrified young woman as the phantom voice resumed the assault on my deteriorating sanity. "John, you have killed for them in foreign lands, spilled blood in defense of their empire, only to be abandoned when your service was no longer required."

The screaming in my mind reached a climax, making vision impossible and rational thought out of question. My headache had intensified to the point where keeping my eyes open required tremendous effort, while my grip on both the scalpel and Miss Kelly grew increasingly unreliable.

Suddenly, hands seized Mary Jane Kelly, wrenching her from my weakening embrace while other arms pinned mine apart. The scalpel rattled to the stone floor as Whitmore's face appeared before mine, wearing an expression of maternal disappointment.

"Now, now, John Watson," she said with mock sympathy. "What are we to do with such behavior?"

I felt the sharp prick of the needle penetrating my neck, followed by the sensation of unknown chemicals entering my bloodstream.

The drug spread through my system with purpose, bringing with it a numbing detachment to separate my consciousness from my physical form.

As the chamber spun around me and darkness closed in from all directions, the last thing I saw was Mary Jane Kelly's terrified face watching my collapse with the wide-eyed horror of someone who had witnessed her own fate sealed. The jasmine scent followed me into unconsciousness, accompanied by the phantom voices as I lost all connection to the waking world.

The city seethed with energy, speaking of impending chaos. The heat of urban unrest had reached a dangerous boiling point, with more citizens filling the streets each day than anyone could remember. What had begun as isolated protests now manifested as daily occurrences at virtually every major intersection, creating a network of discontent spreading like a virus through the body politic.

From Baker Street, I heard the relentless beating of drums, rhythmic pounding to drive rational thought from the mind and replace it with primitive emotion. The sound had become so persistent that even I, accustomed as I was to filtering out urban distractions, found myself growing annoyed more than my usual tolerance.

"Mrs. Hudson!" I yelled out, my voice carrying the sharp edge of irritation, having become increasingly common these past days. "Please remove this meal. I'm entirely without appetite."

My brother, Mycroft, had bolted himself up in the Diogenes Club following our last conversation. However, he had promised to do everything within his power to address what he termed "the current state of affairs." While I possessed great faith in Mycroft's intellectual capabilities—indeed, they exceeded even my own in certain areas—I harbored serious doubts about his ability to extricate himself from the financial web having ensnared him. The conspirators had chosen their target well; Mycroft's pride and ambition had made him the perfect unwitting accomplice. And at this point, both of the personal connections to me were enthralled in this most ingenious conspiracy.

Still, I had to focus my attention, chief among them, on the fate of my dear friend Watson. Private Sloan's intelligence had been invaluable, confirming Watson was not only alive but had been last seen or heading to Warehouse 13 at Lord Barker's estate.

The facts of our case fell into place in my mind like pieces of a complex puzzle, each element connected to the others in ways that became increasingly clear. I threw myself upon the Persian rug before my fireplace, spreading my limbs wide in the position often helping me achieve the mental clarity necessary for complex deduction. The familiar texture of the fabric beneath me, the play of firelight across the ceiling above, the subtle sounds of Mrs. Hudson moving about in the kitchen—all of these sensory details helped anchor my thoughts and prevent them from spiraling into unproductive emotional territory. Somewhere in this tangle of facts lies the key to everything.

The sound of shattering glass interrupted my contemplation with violent suddenness. Debris rained down from my front windows as a brick rolled to a stop mere inches from my head. Mrs. Hudson's screams pierced from the floor below, accompanied by the harsh voices of men meaning harm.

I rolled to my feet, then rushed toward the door while shouting for Mrs. Hudson. Launching myself down the stairs, I arrived at the ground floor to find three rough-looking men attempting to drag my landlady from the building.

"Release her!" I commanded, my voice carrying all the authority I could muster.

The nearest of them faced me, his sneer showing gaps where teeth had been. Before he could respond, I launched myself at him, driving my knee into his solar plexus with enough force to lift him from his feet. As he doubled over, gasping for breath, I spun toward his companion and delivered a perfectly timed uppercut, snapping his head backward and sending him tumbling to the pavement.

The third man, seeing his companions dispatched with such effectiveness, released Mrs. Hudson and fled into the chaos of the street. I gathered my landlady in my arms and guided her quickly inside, slamming the door behind us and sliding the heavy bolt into place.

"Oh, Mr. Holmes," she gasped, her voice trembling with shock and fear. "What is happening to our city? There are so many angry people in the streets—they seem to have lost all reason and decency."

"Secure all the doors and windows, Mrs. Hudson," I instructed while reaching for my hat and coat. "Retreat to the basement and remain there until I return. I fear this is only the beginning of tonight's troubles."

I left Baker Street and plunged into a cityscape drawn straight from the deepest circles of hell itself. Citizens ran in all directions, some fleeing from violence while others actively sought it out. Windows shattered, and fires began to break out at various points throughout the district.

The police, those few brave souls attempting to maintain order, found themselves hopelessly outnumbered. I watched in horror as several constables who tried to blow their whistles for assistance were surrounded by mobs of twenty or more men and beaten senseless. Their colleagues, witnessing such scenes, abandoned their posts and fled to save themselves.

It was during this urban apocalypse I spotted my irregular network of street children. Wiggins and his compatriots had taken shelter in the doorway of a shuttered shop, their young faces filled with the kind of terror no child should ever experience.

"Mr. 'Olmes!" Wiggins called out when he spotted me, his voice barely audible above the surrounding chaos. "What should we do? Where can we go?" The sound of gunfire—sharp, distinct pops—echoed from multiple directions. I instinctively placed myself between the children and the street, using my body to shield them as much as possible.

Kneeling beside Wiggins, I placed my hands on his shoulders and stared into his frightened eyes. "Listen carefully, my boy. I want you to take all the others to the rear entrance of my lodgings. Knock exactly three times, tell Mrs. Hudson I sent you, and she will provide you with safety and sustenance. Can you do this for me?"

All the children nodded with the solemn gravity of youth confronted by genuine danger. They understood their survival might depend on following my instructions precisely.

"Good lads," I said, pointing toward 221B across the chaos of the thoroughfare. "Stay together, move quickly, and look after one another."

I watched as they wove their way through the mob with the agility only children seem to possess, ducking beneath grasping hands and slipping through gaps between bodies until they reached the safety of my building's rear courtyard.

Turning my attention back to the larger crisis, I noticed patterns within the apparent randomness of the violence. While most of the rioters moved in the confused, chaotic manner one would expect from a genuine spontaneous uprising, certain groups displayed a level of organization distinctly out of place.

The men wearing red sashes around their arms—traveling in formation rather than as individuals —and, most significantly, they were heading in the opposite direction from the general flow of fleeing citizens. Where others ran away from the violence, these men moved purposefully toward specific destinations.

They were gathering in increasing numbers around what appeared to be a distribution point in the middle of the street. The wooden crates, the ones I had seen beforehand, were being opened, and torches were passed from man to man in an assembly line. Their coordinated arson campaign was about to begin.

We were now only a single block from Blackheath Hospital, and the targeting seemed far from coincidental. As I watched, fascinated and dread-filled, at least twenty torches were ignited simultaneously. "Trim the tree!" they began chanting in unison, their voices forming a rhythmic war cry that sent chills down my spine. "Make them bleed!"

The torches flew through the air in synchronized arcs, sailing over the hospital's iron fence and through windows, exploding inward under the impact. Within moments, multiple fires had taken hold throughout the building, and the night air filled with the pungent smell of smoke. The evidence of Shepard's psychological experiments was conveniently destroyed.

"Trim the tree!" they continued shouting as they fanned out, their voices creating a cacophony of mayhem designed to inspire panic in anyone who heard it.

As I watched the destruction, one of the red-sashed figures separated from the leading group and stopped at a nearby street corner. He raised his arm, and the red fabric of his sash fluttered in the hot air rising from the burning building. Then he turned, and in the flickering light of the flames, I saw his face.

It was Eddie, the orderly from Blackheath Hospital. He stood motionless, staring directly at me with an expression that combined triumph, malice, and something that might have been pity.

The flames rose higher behind him, framing his silhouette like something from a medieval painting of damnation. London was burning, Watson was lost somewhere in the web of manipulation having ensnared him, and I stood face to face with a man intending to ensure neither my friend nor I survived to see the dawn.

Their revolution, their conspiracy had begun, and I was too late to put a stop to it.

CHAPTER 14

Whisper in the Wires

Their grand plan had succeeded even by my most pessimistic deductions. The forgotten masses of London—those whom society had discarded like used fruit peels—had proven ideally suited to serve as instruments of chaos and calamity. Nearly a week had now passed since the first riots erupted in the far central district, and the city writhed in agony beneath a pall of smoke.

I had tried to steady Mrs. Hudson's nerves, though the constant din of violence past our walls had left her significantly altered. The ir-regulars had transformed themselves into a private guard, watching over both the building and my landlady with the fierce devotion of children protecting a beloved mother. Despite my repeated attempts, I had received no word from Mycroft, nor had I been able to penetrate the official silence surrounding his current circumstances.

By Friday morning, the crowds had thinned somewhat, though the choking smell of burned shops and houses had settled into London's bones. Even the rabble needs a break to find sustenance before their next volley of anarchy and destruction.

A sharp knock at the door interrupted my brooding. My usual practice of observing visitors from the window had been eliminated by vandalism, leaving me to rely on more primitive methods of identification.

"Who calls?" I shouted down.

"Inspector Bradstreet," came the reply from below.

I faced Mrs. Hudson and the boys, all of whom regarded me with apprehension. With a quick gesture, I indicated they should remain in place.

"I shall return directly," I announced, then made my way down to the entrance.

Sliding away the heavy armoire we had used to barricade the door, I found Inspector Bradstreet waiting on the walk with another constable and a police carriage.

"Get in," he stated with intensity, offering no other quip.

"What news, Inspector?" I inquired as we began our journey through what remained of London's districts.

"Heading east, I see."

Bradstreet's face wore the expression of a man who had lost all his empathy. "The rioting and looting is contained for the most part. Her majesty has brought in the military to help us secure the streets. But they found something horrific, Holmes. This latest murder surpasses all the others in cruelty. The victim has been truly slaughtered. In all this chaos the bodies are really piling up." He shifted in his seat to turn away from me. "I just don't know what to do anymore."

"When was the body discovered?"

"This morning, the victim's name is Mary Jane Kelly—she was only twenty years old." His voice dropped to barely above a whisper. "The killer mutilated her face, exceeding recognition, and removed her heart, Holmes... took it."

Weaving through checkpoints and blockades in the street, we arrived at 13 Miller's Court, adjacent to Spitalfields, as the clock struck noon. Two constables stood guard at the building's main entrance, their faces betraying the strain of maintaining composure and keeping watch for a crowd to rise from the street itself.

I stepped down from the carriage to follow Bradstreet inside, but he remained seated, his gaze fixed straight ahead.

"You continue alone, Holmes. I have seen quite enough," he said, settling back against the cushions. "I shall wait here."

Inside the building, I climbed narrow stairs creaking ominously beneath my weight. Another constable waited outside a boarding room door, its surface bearing the accumulated paint of at least four layers, each peeling away to reveal the colors beneath. The door had swollen in its frame, requiring significant force to push it open.

A police photographer was completing his work as I entered, his equipment representing one of Scotland Yard's recent innovations in criminal investigation. The man lifted his camera with obvious haste, covered his mouth with his free hand, and hurried past me toward the corridor. His retreat spoke more eloquently than words about the scene he had been documenting.

I stood alone in the sudden silence, broken only by the distant cooing of doves mocking the horror before me. Sunlight streamed through the single window, casting a path of deceptive warmth across the bed where Mary Jane Kelly lay.

Bradstreet's description had been accurate but insufficient. The young woman's face had been systematically destroyed, sliced, surpassing any possibility of identification. The extreme nature of this mutilation suggested deep personal significance—the killer had been unable or unwilling to look upon her features while he worked, I observed. Perhaps she had reminded him of someone from his past —a mother or sister — whose memory had become entangled with whatever madness drove him to these acts.

The throat wound followed the now-familiar pattern: a single cut from left to right, executed with intent and knowledge. But the abdominal mutilations represented an escalation. The killer had opened her body with the methodical care of a physician conducting an autopsy, removing organs with deliberate precision and arranging them in a grotesque parody of scientific examination.

The missing heart was plainly evident. Unlike the other removed organs, placed with apparent randomness, the heart had been taken away entirely—a trophy, perhaps, or an offering to whatever evil purpose motivated these crimes.

I knelt to examine the floor more closely, noting the impressions left by the killer's boots as he had moved around the bed during his work. The patterns suggested he had spent time at his task, moving with deliberation rather than haste. The fireplace showed evidence of recent use—ashes and debris indicating the killer had stoked the flames to provide additional light for his activities over a period of hours.

This murder differed significantly from the predecessors. While the others had occurred in public spaces or locations where discovery was likely, Mary Jane Kelly had died in the privacy of her own lodgings. The killer had enjoyed unlimited time to complete his work without fear of interruption, indicating either she had known him well enough to admit him voluntarily, or he had gained entry through some other means arousing no suspicion. Not surprising, given the lawlessness of the past week.

Rising from my examination of the fireplace, I brushed the soot from my hands and approached the constable standing guard outside.

"Have any witnesses come forward? Did anyone report unusual sounds during the night?"

"Nothing whatsoever, sir. The landlady became concerned only when Miss Kelly failed to appear for breakfast. Given the chaos of recent days, she worried some misfortune might have befallen the young woman, but she heard nothing suspicious during the night hours."

"Most curious," I murmured, filing this information alongside my other observations.

As I descended the stairs, my thoughts turned to questions of motive and method. Why had this victim received such elaborate attention? What purpose did the theatrical elements serve outside the apparent desire to shock and horrify? The killer had invested time and effort in creating this scene—but for whose benefit?

Outside, I drew several deep breaths of the smoky air, grateful even for its tainted quality after the atmosphere of the death chamber above.

"If you know Watson's whereabouts, Holmes, now would be the time for complete honesty," Bradstreet said, leaning forward in the carriage with an expression of urgent concern.

"Ripper strikes again!" shouted a newspaper boy as he ran past our position.

The lad's presence on the streets surprised me—few children had been venturing out during the recent troubles—but his announcement proved even more remarkable. The murder had occurred only hours earlier, yet already the press had obtained sufficient details to produce headlines.

"I cannot protect his reputation much longer, Holmes," Bradstreet continued. "My superiors are demanding we release Watson's name publicly and organize a comprehensive manhunt. The pressure from above has become... considerable."

The inspector's careful phrasing suggested influences above the normal chain of command. Shepard was orchestrating events, ensuring that Watson would be identified as the perpetrator, regardless of any evidence to the contrary.

"Very well, Inspector. We shall delay no longer. Take us to Lord Barker's estate in Kent."

The approach to Barker's estate revealed changes confirming my worst fears about recent political developments. Military personnel lined the immaculate roadway in formation, their presence transforming what had once been a peaceful country road into something resembling an army encampment. The main gate was guarded by four soldiers in dress uniforms—bright red coats with gold braiding, black trousers pressed to razor sharpness, the bearing of elite units.

One of the guards stepped directly into the path of our horses, raising his hand in the universal signal for immediate halt. Our driver pulled sharply on the reins, bringing the carriage to an abrupt stop, jolting both Bradstreet and myself against the forward bulkhead.

"Who goes there?" the soldier demanded.

"Inspector Bradstreet of Scotland Yard and Mr. Sherlock Holmes," the inspector replied with all the authority his position could muster.

"No admittance permitted," came the flat response.

I rose from my seat and stepped down to the roadway, hoping direct confrontation might prove more effective than Bradstreet's official credentials.

"We are here in search of Dr. John Watson. I demand an immediate audience with Lord Barker."

The remaining three guards moved forward with their rifles at the ready position, effectively blocking any further advance toward the estate.

"No admittance under direct orders of the Prime Minister," the lieutenant stated.

"I shall have you know we are here at the express behest," Bradstreet began.

"Prime Minister Barker has departed for Downing Street," the officer interrupted. "If you require an audience, you must seek him there."

I stepped back into the carriage, exchanging glances with Bradstreet, reflecting our mutual shock at this casual revelation.

"Prime Minister Barker?" I inquired carefully. "What has become of Lord Salisbury?"

"Cannot say, sir. Orders state only Her Majesty has dissolved Parliament and appointed Lord Barker to form a new government. We were dispatched to secure his estate against rioters and other undesirable elements."

"It's finished then." I thought. The conspiracy had achieved the final objectives far beyond mere financial manipulation or even localized civil unrest. They had maneuvered themselves into the highest levels of government, using the chaos they had created as justification for sweeping changes that typically require months of political jostling.

As we traveled back toward London, the extent of the transformation became increasingly apparent. More and more military wagons filled the streets, cavalry patrols moved in formation along major thoroughfares, and transport vehicles discharged armed soldiers at virtually every significant intersection. The city had been placed under complete martial authority.

"New emergency powers must have been declared," Bradstreet observed with unease.

"Indeed. Order must be maintained, regardless of the cost to traditional liberties."

By the time we reached Scotland Yard, even such a bastion of civilian authority had acquired a distinctly military character. Police constables now shared duties with army personnel, while barriers had been erected to control public access to the building. Press crowded the entrance hall, their notebooks plainly evident, awaiting some significant announcement.

Dr. Shepard stood at a podium near the front of the assembly, delivering what appeared to be an official statement regarding recent criminal investigations. His voice carried through the crowded space as he outlined the latest developments in the Whitechapel murders.

"Our primary suspect in these dreadful murders is Dr. John Watson, longtime associate and colleague of Mr. Sherlock Holmes," he announced with theatrical precision.

As he spoke, Shepard pointed directly toward my position at the rear of the hall. At once, every journalist in the room turned toward me with voracious intensity. Questions erupted from multiple angles, creating demands for statements, explanations, and exclusive interviews.

I stood frozen in the sudden glare of public scrutiny, deaf to the specific words being shouted but understanding perfectly the implications of what had occurred. The trap had been sprung with perfect timing, ensuring my association with Watson would taint any defense I might attempt to mount on his behalf.

Shepard smiled directly at me before stepping down from the podium, followed by an entourage of high-ranking police officials and military officers, whose presence underscored the new power structure emerging from the chaos.

Bradstreet grasped my shoulder and guided me firmly toward the exit, shielding me as much as possible from the pursuing mob of reporters. He pushed me into our carriage and instructed the driver to leave, without regard for destination.

I removed my hat and flung it to the floor of the carriage, frustrated. "Elementary, my dear Holmes." I said aloud as I yelled at the driver to make for Baker Street.

"Come along, Doctor. Time to be moving."

Charlie's voice penetrated the fog of my consciousness like sunlight through storm clouds. He grasped my arm and pulled me upright from the narrow cot serving as my bed, though I could not remember lying down or how much time had passed since the last time I was aware of my surroundings.

"Just a moment," I protested, struggling against the sudden brightness assaulting my vision. My spinning head spun with the familiar confusion, becoming my constant companion, making clear thought a luxury.

"Here, Eddie, take charge of him," Charlie called out as the man approached from the shadows outside my restricted field of vision.

"What shall I tell Dr. Shepard?" Charlie asked.

"Tell him Watson has taken flight."

The phrase struck me as significant; it seemed more like a code than actual banter. All my recent days lay veiled in troublesome confusion, the mist lifting only at intervals to reveal brief fragments of clarity.

"Where are you taking me?" I managed to ask as they guided me toward what appeared to be a doorway.

"Here," Eddie said, his voice a low whisper as he helped me put on a rough coat. He pressed something metallic and hard into my palm. I looked down, and my heart ached. It was my bistoury. "Shepard's men took this from your room," Eddie explained, his eyes grim. "They were going to plant it on you for good after... after their work was done. You should have it. A soldier needs his weapon. Quiet now, Doc. We're getting you safe."

The journey that followed defied easy description. I found myself concealed beneath hay in the bed of a wagon, the scratchy, dried grass tickling my nose and threatening to set off sneezing fits, possibly revealing my presence to unwelcome observers. The change from dirt road to cobblestone told me we were entering London, though the wisdom of returning to the city escaped me entirely.

I knew the police sought me for murder. Crimes so horrible my mind recoiled from contemplating them in detail. Yet I could not remember committing such acts. But the gaps in my memory troubled me profoundly. I retained fragments—screams, possibly real or imagined, the sight of blood belonging to battlefield casualties or more recent victims, sensations of violence, feeling both foreign and familiar. My mind contained pieces of a puzzle refusing to form a coherent picture, leaving me uncertain about the most basic facts of recent experience.

The wagon halted inside what sounded like a large, enclosed space—a warehouse, perhaps, judging by the echoing quality of voices and the creak of heavy doors swinging closed behind us. Hands searched for my boots and, finding them, used them to drag me toward the edge of the wagon bed. Other men began clearing away the hay concealing me.

As my vision cleared, I counted roughly ten men gathered around the wagon. All bore the unmistakable marks of military service — posture and careful attention to detail —despite the informal circumstances. These were veterans, men understanding discipline and the importance of following orders even in chaotic situations. Eddie climbed down from the driver's seat and observed me with an expression that mixed concern with determination.

"Out you come, Doc. These lads will see you safely past the city limits."

"Why should I trust any of you?" I asked, though even as I spoke, I recognized the futility of resistance.

"Because, Doctor, you've got no choice. Shepard means to kill you. He has already disposed of Nurse Whitmore—yesterday, as it happens."

The news struck me. "Martha Whitmore is dead? How do you know this?"

"Because I killed her myself," Eddie replied with matter-of-fact simplicity. "She deserved such a fate, Doctor. She was a willing party in Shepard's schemes, gave us the drugs, and messed with our minds. She was evil—corrupted after 'Gany."

"You killed her?" I could barely comprehend what I was hearing.

"I had no choice, Doc. Shepard ordered me to kill you as well, but we couldn't allow it to happen. We served together."

I pressed my hands against my temples, trying to organize thoughts and find patterns to reason. The deductive principles Holmes taught me were beginning to scatter like leaves in the wind. "But the wom en... the screams I remember... please tell me I did not commit those murders."

"Shepard and Whitmore manipulated all of us, Doctor, using us as instruments for their purposes. But you helped us—you altered medications, replaced their drugs with harmless substances, and found ways to preserve our sanity even while appearing to cooperate with their experiments. You saved us, so now we're returning the favor."

One of the men approached with a newspaper, the headline visible even from a distance: "WATSON WANTED—WHEREABOUTS UNKNOWN."

The sight of my name in such a context filled me with despair. "Dear God... where is Holmes? I must speak with him."

"Cannot say where he might be found, but he'll manage well enough on his own. We must get you away from here. Lord Barker has become Prime Minister and deployed military forces specifically to hunt you down. This river boat represents our only chance—upstream passage to the north country."

"Allow me to write a letter," I pleaded. "One moment, I beg you."

Eddie hurried to an office within the warehouse and returned with paper and a pencil. "Be quick about it, Doc. Every minute increases our danger."

I closed my eyes, attempting to gather my scattered thoughts into some form of coherent communication.

My Dear Holmes:

I find myself compelled to offer the sincerest apologies for the troubles my circumstances have brought upon you. I should have sought your counsel much earlier regarding Bailey's death and my discoveries concerning Dr. Shepard's activities. I deeply regret you must now bear the weight of public speculation and official suspicion.

I can state with complete honesty I possess no clear recollection of committing the crimes attributed to me. The treatments administered by Dr. Shepard and Nurse Whitmore involved systematic drugging not only of myself but of numerous other veterans as well. These men are now assisting my escape, though I cannot say where our journey will lead or when circumstances might permit my return.

Guard yourself carefully, my dear friend. The forces arrayed against us possess resources and influence.

Your devoted companion, John H. Watson

I folded the paper carefully and wrote the address of 221B Baker Street on the reverse side.

"Promise me this will reach Mr. Sherlock Holmes without delay."

"You have my word, Doc. Now into the boat—we must depart while darkness provides concealment."

Several of the other men joined us in the small river craft, their presence providing some measure of security as we pushed away from the warehouse dock. The city spread before us like a vision of apocalypse—smoke rising from countless fires, the skeletal remains of burned buildings, the distant sound of military equipment moving through streets once knowing peace.

"What devastation," I murmured as I settled onto a bench within the boat's small cabin. "The entire city appears to have been destroyed."

"You don't know the half of it, Doc," one of the men replied grimly. "Keep down and stay quiet until we're well clear of the city."

I lay back against the wooden seat and closed my eyes, drawing the first deep breath I had managed in what felt like months. Despite the uncertainty of our destination and the gravity of accusations hanging over me, I felt something approaching peace for the first time since this nightmare had begun.

Whatever Shepard and his associates had done to my mind was finally beginning to loosen its hold, allowing fragments of my true self to resurface from beneath layers of artificial confusion and manufactured guilt.

The boat moved steadily upstream, carrying me away from London and toward whatever refuge awaited in the northern territories—but also toward the possibility of reclaiming my identity and discovering the truth about the crimes nearly destroying everything I held dear.

CHAPTER 15

The Last Letter

I n the quiet of our sitting room, I found myself remembering the first time I learned how minor oversights could have devastating consequences. When I was but a boy of ten, a cousin, Reginald, came to summer with our family. He brought along his dog Victor—a Scottish Collie with beautiful, long tan and white hair, gentle in temperament, and devoted.

My father sternly warned Reginald to ensure the garden gate remained properly latched, and all summer, Mycroft would loyally secure it behind us after our adventures in the countryside. Reginald never bothered with such insurances, far too interested in butterfly collecting and botanical sketches, too preoccupied with pursuits he deemed more worthy of his attention. This carelessness continued until the night of the great storm, when Mycroft wasn't with us and the gate went unlatched. The wind seized upon the oversight with violent enthusiasm, flinging the barrier wide and allowing Victor to race into the wild darkness, terrified by the thunder and lightning splitting the sky above our estate. We found him two days later, drowned in the bog in the west pasture, his beautiful coat matted with mud and his loyal eyes staring sightlessly at the gray morning sky.

I remember how quiet the house became after the discovery. Mycroft never spoke a word of reproach, though the weight of responsibility settled upon his young shoulders. It was Reginald's fault, certainly, but it was also mine. I had seen the gate, known the importance, and failed to ensure its security.

The tragedy taught me life's most dangerous elements aren't the storms themselves. They are the things we leave undone, the words unsaid, the doors unlatched, the loose ends fluttering in the wind until disaster claims them. This lesson has guided my career as a consulting detective, as an intellectual, and as a man who values honor above convenience. It explains why I tie every knot, answer every question, and chase every whisper until its source stands revealed. Everything unlatched will eventually escape—and when it does, the consequences rarely limit themselves to the careless party alone. My mind, an engine constructed for dissecting the most intricate puzzles, finds no peace until every cog engages properly and every spring accounts for itself.

Yet here I sit, decades later, contemplating another gate left unlatched, another friend endangered by my failures.

Watson's red velvet chair sat empty before me in our familiar sitting room, calling like a memorial to a now-endangered friendship. The afternoon light streaming through our windows was different somehow—thinner, more fragile, as though recent events had altered the atmosphere. I had already consumed three pipes during my contemplation, the tobacco's familiar ritual offering little comfort. My study was a maelstrom of scattered facts and disconnected clues. Shepard, the veterans, the Ripper murders, the opium, Mycroft's financials, shipping manifests, Operation Fawkes—all were pieces of a grand and monstrous design.

The irregulars maintained their vigil outside our door. At the same time, Mrs. Hudson busied herself with unnecessary tidying—both activities serving to mask the anxiety settled over 221B Baker Street like morning fog. The distant sounds of military patrols echoed through streets once known for the peaceful rhythms of commercial life, reminding us all how the world had fundamentally changed. Every few minutes, the clip-clop of horses and the sound of boots as another squadron passed on the sidewalk. London had become an occupied city, and I had failed to prevent it.

The conspirators had played us masterfully, but how? What was the central principle? My preoccupation with the India Treasure Case had been a fatal error —a diversion that allowed the actual threat to fester. The amateur theatrics at the pawnshop, the timing of Private Bailey's death—they were all too perfect, too clean.

It was this maddening perfection tormenting me. Crime, in its essence, is a human endeavor, and humanity is defined by imperfections. A true criminal enterprise should have frayed edges, moments of chance, untidy loose ends. This conspiracy had none. It was a flawless construct, an orchestrated reality, and, more than anything else, it pointed to a single, terrifying intelligence at its heart—an intelligence I had contemplated before.

The sharp ring of our doorbell tore through my brooding.

Mrs. Hudson's hurried footsteps on the stairs announced a visitor of some urgency, though her manner suggested apprehension. "Mr. Holmes," she called breathlessly as she entered the sitting room, "This arrived for you."

She extended a letter bearing my name in Watson's familiar handwriting, along with our Baker Street address. Hope, a lost sensation so foreign it felt like poison, surged through me. The paper showed signs of hasty composition—slight tremors in the lettering, speaking of emotional strain and limited time for careful penmanship.

"Who delivered this correspondence?" I inquired, moving to the window to peer down at the street below. The lamplighters would be making their rounds soon, though their work was almost quaint in a city now patrolled by armed soldiers.

"A strange fellow, sir. Couldn't get a proper look at his face, but he wore an eye patch and spoke with a thick Scottish accent. Seemed nervous-like, kept glancing over his shoulder."

I examined the letter with growing unease. The writing was indeed Watson's—I knew every quirk of his penmanship as well as I knew my own—but something felt strange about the entire delivery. The timing arrived precisely when my desperation peaked. Watson had been missing for more than two months; for a rescue message to surface now suggested either remarkable luck or careful calculation.

Still, I had to follow this thread, regardless of where it might lead. The alternative was paralysis, and this note bore Watson's handwriting, not a failed attempt to copy it.

"Thank you, Mrs. Hudson. Please ask the Irregulars to maintain their watch, but with increased caution. If anything feels amiss, they should retreat rather than investigate."

As she left the room, I studied the letter more closely under the lamplight. The paper bore faint traces of river water, the pungent smell of fish and coal smoke—details easily fabricated, but my desperate mind seized upon them as evidence of possible authenticity. The creases suggested it had been folded hastily and carried in someone's pocket. If this was deception, it was masterfully crafted, playing upon my own methods of deduction to guide me toward a predetermined conclusion.

But what choice did I have? Even knowing this might be a trap, I had to pursue it.

"To Millbank Pier!" I called, hailing a cab. If Watson were truly being moved by river, the government docks in Westminster, near Parliament, would be the logical departure point—close enough to the seat of power for official boats, yet busy enough to mask unusual activity.

The journey required careful navigation around military barricades. The cabbie, a grizzled veteran of London's streets, navigated the obstacles with practiced skill while muttering under his breath about "foreign ways on English soil."

At Millbank Pier, I found the typical evidence of boat traffic, but as I questioned the dock workers, a horrible certainty began to form.

Their answers were lines of a play, rehearsed for my benefit. The laborer who described a steam launch heading north with military men aboard spoke with exactness. He knew exactly how many men were aboard, could explain their leader's eye patch in remarkable detail, and even recalled overhearing fragments of conversation about "safe houses in the northern counties."

The timing aligned precisely with the letter's delivery. Even the description of the leader's appearance—as though the same person crafting one part of the deception had been unable to resist leaving his signature on another.

I was being led by the nose, guided through a carefully constructed illusion using my own deductive methods against me. Someone who understood my mind intimately had crafted this elaborate charade, knowing I would analyze the physical evidence, knowing I would reach the Thames, knowing I would find these convenient witnesses telling me exactly what I needed to hear.

Standing at the pier's edge, watching the muddy water flow past the great monuments of British power—Parliament, Westminster Abbey, the heart of our empire—I felt the noose closing in around my neck. This entire exercise had been designed to consume precious time while giving me the illusion of progress.

There was only one mind capable of such intricate psychological manipulation, one intellect having studied me closely enough to predict my every response and turn my greatest strengths into weapons against me.

I returned to Baker Street, my brief hope extinguished and replaced by ominous certainty. The architect wished me to know my every move was anticipated, my every strength bent to their purpose, my thoughts manipulated like pieces on a chessboard.

The worst part was its elegance. This conductor created a scenario in which my own deductive abilities led me to the correct conclusion—I was being deceived—while simultaneously leaving me powerless to do anything about it. It was psychological warfare of the highest order.

I climbed the steps to our flat, each one feeling heavier than the last. Mrs. Hudson met me at the door; her face creased with worry.

"Any word of the good doctor, sir?"

"Not yet, Mrs. Hudson. But we may have visitors this evening. Perhaps you might consider spending the night with your sister in Paddington?"

Her expression sharpened with understanding. "Of course, but there's a man here. You have a visitor in your study." She pointed down the hall at the door and started down the steps. "I'll gather my things at once, Mr. Holmes. But are you certain you don't need—"

"Quite certain. This is a matter requiring resolution between the parties directly involved."

She nodded and hurried away. I sauntered down the hall, opened the door to our sitting room, and stopped dead.

"Good afternoon, Mr. Holmes," Seated in my chair, silhouetted against the firelight, was a man of elegant clothing and style. "I hope you don't mind. Dear Mrs. Hudson, was kind enough to let me in."

The sight of this man troubled me greatly—tall, pale, with dark eyes to see through flesh and bone to the very soul beneath.

"It is a great pleasure to meet you, finally, Mr. Holmes," he said as he extended his hand. I shook it firmly. "My name is..."

"Professor James Moriarty," I said bluntly, interrupting him. It could only be the spider at the heart of the web. Previous cases had led me to believe someone was orchestrating them. Moriarty had done considerable work to eliminate any trace of his name or involvement, but I had deduced it on a few occasions.

We stood facing each other in the flickering firelight, two adversaries having played this game before. He began to move, circling the room with predatory grace, and I found myself matching his movements, two warriors taking measure of one another in the familiar arena of my sitting room.

"This case—unique in the annals of crime, wouldn't you agree? Ingenious and well designed," he began with evident satisfaction, trailing one gloved finger along the mantelpiece as he passed. "Please, indulge me, Sherlock Holmes, Consulting Detective. Explain how you believe this was all accomplished."

The request was both an invitation and an ambush. He wanted to hear me unravel this masterpiece, to demonstrate my understanding while simultaneously revealing my helplessness. But what choice did I have? Perhaps, in the telling, I might notice an overlooked weakness, a thread capable of being pulled to unravel his design.

"The true artistry was not the coup itself, but the misdirection preceding it. You began with the veterans—broken men whose minds had been shattered by war and reformed by the good doctor Shepard into malleable instruments of your will."

"A pitiable and pliable resource," Moriarty interjected with a thin smile holding no warmth. "The mind, when properly broken, can be rebuilt to serve almost any purpose. Please continue."

"You used them to create your crisis, but with multiple layers of purpose. The Ripper murders served to eliminate witnesses from your opium network—women who might have identified your agents or your financial backers. They doubly created public hysteria demanding government action, giving fuel to a fire and providing the perfect pretext for military intervention. But most importantly, they delivered the perfect frame for Watson."

I paused, watching his face for any reaction. He gave none, merely nodding encouragingly as though I were a promising student working through a complex theorem.

"You chose Simon Bailey specifically because you knew Watson's involvement with him and his compassionate nature would compel his involvement. A veteran was murdered, with evidence suggesting he had sought help from a doctor. Watson could no more ignore such a case than he could have stopped breathing."

"His devout loyalty is his greatest weakness," Moriarty purred, moving to examine my violin case with insincere curiosity. "As is yours, of course. The great Sherlock Holmes, brought low by something so simple as human affection."

"The planted evidence in Bailey's coat, the paid-off pawnbroker who identified a woman, Nurse Whitmore's convenient arrival—all theater designed to guide him into your web. But the true genius was the timing." My voice grew tighter as the full scope of his manipulation became clear. "You arranged for this frame-up to occur while I was distracted by the India Treasure Case, knowing my obsessive nature would prevent me from seeing the larger pattern until it was too late."

Moriarty abandoned the violin and moved to the window, gazing out at the street below. "The India case was indeed fortuitous. The sweet Mary Morstan required a terrific sum to bring you the case. Though I confess, I may have provided certain... encouragements... to ensure it captured your full attention at this crucial moment. A few carefully planted clues, nothing too obvious, of course."

I stood up and walked toward him with clenched fists, but relaxed my hands. "Then there is the coup and her majesty's government."

"Yes, well, that was the easiest part of the entire scheme. Politicians are ruthless people, willing to sell their own mothers for more power and wealth. I had to promise them very little." He moved towards me and put Watson's chair between us. "I had more fun in twisting your cases and your games."

The casual admission hit me like a slap across my face. Even the Agra India case, my supposed triumph, had been orchestrated to serve his purposes. I was not the master detective I had believed myself to be, but a puppet dancing on strings so subtle I had never felt their pull.

"The scope of it all, the psychological sophistication, the perfect ti ming..." I forced myself to meet his eyes. "It bears your unmistakable signature, Professor. The Napoleon of Crime."

Moriarty let out a brittle laugh, breaking on the air. "What is it you say to dear Watson? Elementary—Yes, elementary, my dear Holmes.

I have been here since you started. A man of my resources, my preparation, watching, waiting, building this grand design while you solved your little cases and basked in public adulation."

He faced away from the window, and in the firelight, his face appeared demonic. "Every criminal you caught, every mystery you solved, every triumph you celebrated—all of it served my purposes. You were the perfect distraction, the brilliant detective whose successes drew attention away from my true work. Do you know how many schemes I completed while the world watched you chase shadows?"

My entire career, everything I had built, every life I thought I had saved—all of it had been part of this larger game. I was not his nemesis but his unwitting accomplice, a performer in a show whose true purpose I had never understood.

"But you have missed the final act," he continued, approaching Watson's chair with predatory intent. "Tell me, Holmes, did you enjoy your excursion to Millbank Pier this afternoon?"

The question confirmed my fear. "You orchestrated the entire charade."

"Every detail. The convenient witnesses with their rehearsed stories, the physical evidence designed to exploit your own methods against you. I needed to demonstrate something important before we concluded our business."

He leaned against the chair's armrest, looming over me with casual dominance. "You believe yourself to be the master of deduction, the great reasoner capable of unraveling any mystery. But I am the architect of your thoughts, Holmes. Every conclusion you reached today was one I placed in your mind. Your greatest strength has become your most exploitable weakness."

"Take the letter out of your front pocket," he demanded. I withdrew the letter from my coat.

He walked over to me and took Watson's letter from my hand and let it drift to the floor. Then, with a deliberate motion, he drove the metal tip of his cane through the center of the page. He moved his cane with the impaled letter and held it inches from my face. The single, clean puncture was a brutal violation.

"You have unraveled the plot, but you have missed the epilogue," he hissed. "Dr. Watson is indeed out of the city and my guest," Moriarty said softly. "The good doctor still believes in fairy tales where the hero arrives in time to save the day."

"What do you want?" The words came out as a whisper.

"Your complete and irrevocable withdrawal from public life," he replied with businesslike factuality. "No more cases, no more investigations, no more interference in matters beyond your concern. You will announce your retirement and retreat to some quiet country cottage where you can tend bees or write memoirs no one will publish."

"And in return?"

"Dr. Watson lives. I may even let you visit each other occasionally, sharing tea and reminiscing about the old days when you believed yourselves important."

The mockery in his voice was unmistakable. He wasn't offering retirement; he was promising a living death, the slow strangulation of everything giving my existence meaning. I would become a ghost haunting my former life, watching the world transform according to his vision while I sat powerless to intervene.

"You're assuming I value Watson's life more than the fate of the Empire."

"Oh, but I know you do." Moriarty's smile was razor-thin. "I know you, Holmes. I know exactly what you value and in what order. Your friend's life matters more to you than any abstract concept of justice or nationalism. It's both your greatest strength and your ultimate vulnerability."

He straightened, smoothing his coat with casual elegance. "And if friendship proves insufficient motivation, consider your brother Mycroft's position in this new order. Government officials who resist change often find their circumstances... diminished. Accidents happen, even to men in the highest positions. My new regime will need to demonstrate authority somehow."

The threat was delivered with such casual politeness it took a moment for its full weight to register. He wasn't only threatening Watson; he was threatening everyone I cared about, everyone who might matter enough to make me act against his interests.

"You have twenty-four hours to consider my proposition," he continued, moving toward the door with unhurried confidence. "After that, Dr. Watson's usefulness as leverage expires, and I will be forced to find other means of ensuring your cooperation."

He paused at the threshold, his hand on the doorknob. "I do hope you'll make the sensible choice, Holmes. It would be such a waste to destroy you entirely when diminishment serves my purposes so much better."

The door closed behind him with a soft click, like the sealing of a coffin. For a moment, the silence pressed in on me, heavier than any storm. He believed he had won. He thought I would retreat into quiet irrelevance, a ghost of my former self.

But I know better than most how even the smallest gate, left unlatched, can change the course of a life. Moriarty has built his empire upon precision, upon perfect control. Yet no design is flawless—no web without a loose thread.

And so, with Watson's life hanging in the balance, I swore I would find the thread—and pull until the entire edifice came crashing down. This was only the beginning.

END OF BOOK ONE

The adventure will continue as Holmes races to find Watson and expose Moriarty's agents and their terrible work...

Afterword

When I first read the adventures of Sherlock Holmes, I was struck not only by his brilliance but by the steady presence of Dr. John Watson. Watson has always been more than a narrator — he is the grounding force, the loyal friend, the man who carries his own burdens yet never falters at Holmes's side.

In *The Shattered Doctor*, I wanted to explore a different side of their relationship. What happens when Watson himself is caught at the center of a mystery? What if the steadfast chronicler of Holmes's triumphs becomes the subject of suspicion, doubt, and danger? This story was born from those questions — and from my belief that even the strongest among us carry unseen wounds.

As someone who has spent a career in fire and emergency services, I have seen how memory, trauma, and loyalty can shape a person. Watson's struggles mirror the quiet battles many endure reconciling the past, protecting their integrity, and leaning on friendship when strength alone is not enough.

I am deeply grateful you chose to spend your time in these pages. If you found this tale worthy of Holmes and Watson's legacy, I would be honored if you shared it with another reader or left a review. It is your support that keeps these timeless characters alive for future generations.

If you'd like to follow my work, including future Holmes stories and my writing on leadership and resilience, please visit me at TwoDar kThirty.com.

Thank you for reading, and for keeping company with two of literature's most enduring friends.

— *Marc Hill*

If you enjoyed The Shattered Doctor...

Please Consider Leaving an Honest Review

Thank you for choosing to spend your time with Sherlock Holmes and Dr. Watson! I sincerely hope you were thoroughly entertained by this latest mystery. The best way you can support independent authors and ensure new adventures are written is by sharing your feedback.

Even a few words can make a huge difference:

- Did you love the suspense?

- Did you enjoy the classic atmosphere of the case?

- Did you feel satisfied by the ending?

Your honest rating and review helps other readers discover The Shattered Doctor on Amazon and across all platforms.

It takes less than a minute!

Visit the book's page on Amazon

1. Scroll down to the Customer Reviews section.

2. Click the button to Write a Customer Review or Rate This
   Product.

Thank you again for reading and for your kind support!

Glossary of Terms & References

221B Baker Street – The famous fictional residence of Sherlock Holmes and Dr. Watson. In this story, it serves as their home base and sanctuary amid chaos.

Second Anglo-Afghan War – From 1878 to 1880 between the British Empire (from its base in India) and Afghanistan, primarily driven by the "Great Game," a geopolitical rivalry to counter Russian influence in Central Asia.

5th Northumberland Fusiliers – A real British Army regiment in which Dr. Watson served. Their involvement in the Second Anglo-Afghan War connects several characters.

Battle of Maiwand – A historical 1880 battle in Afghanistan where Watson was injured. It plays heavily into his trauma and hallucinations.

Blackheath Hospital – A fictionalized veterans' care facility in London, used as a front for psychological manipulation and experimental trauma treatment.

Bistoury Knife – A historical surgical blade used by military doctors like Watson. Its unique striations become key forensic evidence.

Brookton Freight – A fictitious company used to transport illicit and revolutionary materials tied to Moriarty's larger plan.

The Pruners – A secretive group of ex-soldiers and disenfranchised individuals manipulated into becoming agents of chaos. Their insignia is a dead tree with roots exposed.

Operation Fawkes – A covert revolutionary plot designed to incite mass riots and destabilize the British government.

The Ripper Letters – Based on real letters sent to the press during the 1888 Whitechapel murders. In this version, they are tools of misinformation created by Shepard's inner circle.

Jasmine – A symbolic scent tied to trauma and manipulation. It recurs in Watson's dreams and during key moments of psychosis.

Laudanum – An addictive tincture of opium, it is a solution of opium and alcohol, that was historically used as a painkiller and sedative.

About the author

Marc Hill is a retired teacher, and firefighter/paramedic from Wausau Wisconsin. He is an avid reader and fan of Sherlock Holmes and loves the writings of Sir Arthur Conan Doyle along with the Granada series of the Adventures of Sherlock Holmes staring Jeremy Brett, the BBC's Sherlock staring Benedict Cumberbatch, and the Robert Downey Jr. Sherlock Holmes movies.

www.ingramcontent.com/pod-product-compliance
Lightning Source LLC
Chambersburg PA
CBHW022108240626
47153CB00007B/2287